the MIRACLE
of MYSTERIA

the MIRACLE of MYSTERIA

LEONID BELOV

2nd Edition

TRANSLATED BY JOHN MEREDIG
EDITED AND ADAPTED BY THOMAS WOMACK

TOWER OF HARMONY

THE MIRACLE OF MYSTERIA
2nd Edition

Published by Tower of Harmony
132 Sweetgum Road
Peachtree City, Georgia 30269, USA
Email: Contact@TowerOfHarmony.com

Printed in the United States of America.
21 20 19 18 17 16   2 3 4 5
ISBN-13: 978-0-9965513-4-2
ISBN-10: 0-9965513-4-4

Cover Design by Brian Ring Design
Executive Editor: Michael (Misha) Shengaout

This story is inspired by the true events in the
village of Oberammergau, Bavaria, Germany.

Originally published in Russian as:
Мистерия о Страстях Господних
Леонид Белов
Copyright © Леонид Белов, 2006

To my spiritual mentor, pilgrim on the roads of the Divine Wisdom, Blessed Fr. John (Bereslavsky), without whom this book would not be possible.

Contents

Chapter 1
Year of the Black Plague

"WE ALL WALK," the saying goes, "under God's heaven; our lives are in the hands of the Lord." It's something our people have become so accustomed to hearing, they cease thinking about it. Nobody questions it. Nobody gives it a second thought.

Then someone dies—at which time, those remaining will recite: "The Lord gives, and the Lord takes away." Yet their lives go on unchanged. Only if the death is sudden and un-expected will they be frightened into paying full attention. Even that isn't for long. So quickly they move on with a shrug: *Whatever must be, must be; it's all in the Lord's hands.*

I, however, am convinced that much more depends upon you and me in this matter than we realize.

The Lord in his mercy revealed this to me when I was twenty years old—which is a fact, something as certain as the truth of my having reached age eighty-eight, and that I write these words in the city of Geneva in the year of our Lord 1416. Sixty-eight years ago this revelation to me took place— in the Year of the Black Plague.

It happened in the Swiss Alps, in the village where I was born: Rundschau, in the District of Rundschau, Canton of Schwarzwald. At the time of my youth, hardly three hun-dred people lived in our village. Not many more than that live there even now—though if not for the Lord's mercy, most likely not a single living soul would be left.

But I'm getting ahead of myself.

Rundschau is our district's capital, but only because the

surrounding villages (of which there are many) are even smaller. We have a town square with the parish church and town hall, just as you'd find in any proper town; still, it's only a village.

All around this village, nature is rich and bountiful, by the grace of the Lord. Rising slopes are adorned by creeks and waterfalls whose flow is pure, delicious and cold. Meadows are bordered by forests of beech and pine and fir, full of wild game. In higher elevations, one finds sheep farms; in the valleys, wheat is grown and cattle are raised.

Since our district is encompassed on three sides by mountain ranges, there's only one main road; it goes directly through Rundschau village toward Linden, and across the Schwarzwald valley, across Switzerland, and on to Rome itself.

There in Rundschau I was born, in the year 1328, to a family of good Christians. That's what most people in our village considered themselves to be—"good Christians"—right up until that very outbreak of the black plague. Being a good Christian meant weekdays of earning one's daily bread by the sweat of one's brow, weeknights of drinking away those earnings in Rundschau's tavern, Saturdays of beating one's wife, then going to church on Sundays to partake of the body of Christ. It meant remembering: "Do not steal," "Do not kill."

It meant living like everyone else.

Just as with life and death, so also with the subject of what constitutes true Christianity: people of Rundschau preferred not to give it much thought. They each thought they'd been living a godly life from their very birth. But in the year of our Lord 1348, when the black plague entered our land, the events that followed opened everyone's eyes.

When my mind goes back to that time, I try piecing together exactly how God used those events to bring about our new understanding. For some, the explanation starts by assuming that the plague was God's instrument to shake our souls, to punish his children and set them straight. Learned clerics expressed it this way, and most people took their words on faith without question.

To me, however—if I may be so blunt—that answer is unfair to the nature of our merciful Lord. Yes, I'm only the unschooled son of a harness-maker, but I've often heard how our Lord is compared to a shepherd, and we to his sheep. Lothar, my closest friend, had been tending sheep since childhood, and since I often helped him in his work, I became fairly good at caring for a flock. One thing I learned is that punishing alone will not get you far. In fact, it frequently causes more harm than good. What's better is to get the sheep following you on their own—which happens only if they've come to know you, specifically your good side. Then you can guide them with only your voice and the sound of your piping; you rarely if ever have to resort to your shepherd's hook.

One afternoon, two of our sheep got lost. It was nearly nightfall when my friend Lothar and I finally found them in a remote and twisting ravine. The poor things were bleating anxiously and thrashing about. Lothar did exactly what any good shepherd must: he plunged into the ravine and called out their names. The sheep rushed toward the familiar voice. Lothar embraced them, kissed them on their snouts, and whispered comforting words in their ears. On our way back in the darkness, those sheep stayed as close as if they were roped to us.

And so it was, I think, with Rundschau's frightened villagers when our Good Shepherd came to our rescue—though we scarcely imagined this when the plague erupted in our district, bringing terror-filled air, and wagons on the road full of refugees and corpses, and the utter failure of the doctors' heroic efforts to halt death's march.

All of which came so unexpectedly.

It was years later before I learned more about the plague's beginnings. It was said (and I'm inclined to believe it) that the plague came by way of the Genoese and their trading outposts far off on the Eastern Seas. There in the East a great famine befell some nomadic tribes in 1347, and the Genoese took advantage of this to buy up the nomads' children for a pittance, then sell them into slavery at many times the price—some to Turkey, some to Egypt, some to Moorish Spain and Africa. This was undoubtedly a great abomination in the eyes of the Lord, and his vengeance was swift.

These nomads, it so happens, had been subjects of the Emperor of the Mongols, who was enraged when he learned what the merchants had done. He sent an army to besiege the Genoese in their easternmost fortress at Caffa, which was deemed impregnable. The defenders were certain of their stronghold's invincibility; the Lord judged otherwise. Plague suddenly flared up inside the encircled city. Caffa quickly surrendered; the surviving Genoese rushed homeward to Europe, but it was already too late: the epidemic traveled with them.

Port cities were the first to fall. Before the first Genoese ships landed on the Italian shore, the plague already raged in Constantinople and Sicily. Waves of refugees streamed inland along the roads, spreading the pestilence everywhere. There seemed to be no escape.

For the person afflicted, it went like this: he would feel a slight malaise, which suddenly transformed into terrible fever and weakness. Hard nodules would swell under the arms, in the groin, on the throat, in the elbow joints. Dark spots would appear on the face. Diarrhea and vomiting would ensue. Death came within three days.

We in Rundschau heard of these things; soon our talk was of hardly anything else. A scourge of the Lord had been sent to earth to remind us: the cup of our sin has overflowed.

Looking back, I think this was only fair, for is it not better for the one living in sin to die from plague than to keep sinning without repentance for a hundred years? How unwisely we fail to take into account the eternity awaiting us!

Across every land the plague fell, and no one knew how to combat it. Doctors, trying to relieve the victims' suffering, succumbed to the disease themselves. Rulers ordered troops to block borders and roads so no one could leave infected areas, but refugees escaped through forests and over mountains, spreading the affliction ever farther. It reached the palaces of the rulers themselves, to consume them along with their families. The nobleman and the beggar alike trembled before this unprecedented invasion of death; all were equally helpless before it.

Throughout the early months of 1348, rumors made their way to Rundschau of entire cities wiped out in neighboring nations. Our Switzerland lies far from the wasted seaports and plains, but in time the calamity would surely threaten our mountain homeland as well. In summer, when the plague reached Paris, our authorities ordered the Swiss borders closed. Almost immediately, the infection flared up in Lausanne. Our authorities were too late.

Still, we in Rundschau and nearby cantons were the most protected by the Alps. If we were destined to suffer the same fate as everyone else, at least we'd be last in line.

Early in September news arrived that Zurich and Bern were infected, then Geneva, then Lucerne, Uri, Schwyz. By mid-September, Unterwalden and Basel had fallen.

In Rundschau, some of our villagers who returned from travel beyond our district's borders reported roads jammed with refugees. They'd seen corpses lying along the road; had these died from the plague, or simply from exhaustion and starvation?

It was still September when the first refugees appeared in Rundschau—they didn't actually stay with us, but moved farther upland, as if to let the mountains hide them from the wrath of God.

Then one day Johann Holgert—our mayor and district judge, the most educated man in our village, who'd graduated from the University of Bologna—returned from administrative business in the neighboring district. His face ashen, he spoke to us in a quavering voice: "The plague is in Linden."

Chapter 2
Action Like a Man

ON THE DAY AFTER Judge Holgert's news, the flow of refugees through Rundschau ceased. One of our villagers went out to investigate; he discovered that overnight, armed Canton Guards had cordoned the Linden-Rundschau road, sealing off nearby forests and blocking every intersecting byway. Since this was the only road into our district—surrounded as we are by mountains—we were as tightly sealed as a corked bottle.

If this quarantine's success had been the will of God, we might have waited out the plague without further alarm. But the Lord ordained otherwise.

In those days, in the attic where my little brother Thomas and I slept, we overheard an exchange between my mother, who wept with terror, and my father, who at first only sighed. (Although I'm eighty-eight years old, my memory of these things remains sharp.) Suddenly my father said, "How can we sit here like rabbits in a hole, shutting the whole world out?"

"What else would you do?" my mother cried. "Go to Linden and catch your death along with everyone there? Don't think of it! I won't let you! And neither will the guards."

Father, unlike his usual self, did not snap back at her. He sighed. "Oh, God—what indeed can we do?"

September's final day came and went with nothing having passed through the cordon—neither refugee nor rumor. Already folks in Rundschau raised their hopes that the plague might pass us by.

The next morning—Wednesday, October first—a woman with disheveled clothing and hair came running into our village. It was Bertha Zellermann from Waldheim, a sheep farm high in the mountains. She was the wife of Zellermann the hunter, who often came into our village. Bertha seemed out of her mind, capable only of sobbing.

After much trying, Mama Bremer, the miller's wife, managed to calm her enough to utter anything coherent. Amid tears, Bertha spilled her terrible news: the plague had reached Waldheim.

Here is what we managed to piece together from her words. Ten days earlier, their little settlement—three dwellings that housed sixteen people—was visited by a family of distant Zellermann relatives fleeing the plague, having come with their cart all the way from Geneva. Zellermann the hunter took them in. Within three days, he and two of his sons (Kurt and Klaus—I knew them both, and Klaus was my age), as well as all three of the new arrivals, were bedridden in a plague-induced delirium. Zellermann was the first to die. Very soon the plague spread to the others there.

By the end of the week, which had passed so quietly in Rundschau, the new widow, nearly beside herself with grief, took off running down the trail. She did not look back at the terrible sight of Waldheim, where the farm's dogs howled, and the unfed sheep were bleating. There had been time and strength to bury only three of the plague's victims; fifteen other bodies still remained unburied inside the three houses.

We in Rundschau were all dumbfounded by her story. Our last hope of being spared came crashing down. The armed cordon around the district had not saved us.

Now there would be no distinction between "us" and "them," between inside and outside. The plague was everywhere. Already its black mask seemed to stare into all our windows.

Despite our terror, the village of Rundschau did not turn Bertha away. Anna-Katerina Krause, a wizened old midwife living by herself on the edge of the village, agreed to take her in.

My father that day gave me permission to go into the mountains. I wanted to see Lothar, who at first light had taken his flock to graze in the last autumn meadows. I found him at our favorite spot along the Kreuzbach brook, where the grass was still green. To Lothar I blurted out everything I'd heard about Waldheim. His eyes seemed almost to pop from his head.

I watched him closely. Lothar glanced restlessly over the sheep; they grazed around the Kreuzbach waterfall, blissfully unaware of the plague. He looked up at well-chosen spots higher up where his three shepherd dogs, of good Alpine breed, stood guard over the meadow.

Finally Lothar spoke. With embarrassment, he confessed his urge to take off running from Rundschau and not look back. But where could he go?

Lothar looked at me. His right hand made the sign of the cross, spanning head and chest and shoulders. I realized he was preparing himself to die.

The two of us sat side by side under a solitary beech tree on the yellowing Alpine slope. Lothar and I were both twenty years old. Generally speaking, we were no strangers to death. Even in the best of times, there were many in Rundschau who died young, leaving to their friends a sad experience of the inevitability of loss: "Yes, we used to play with Franz Zitterbau, and—well, then he died." At age thirteen, Franz had fallen off a roof and broken his back.

Lothar and I had many such memories. Karl Buntmann, having gone into the mountains to gather wood, died in an avalanche at age twelve. Dora Schneider died of scarlet fever at seven; Lieschen Schneebau and Kaspar Licht, both six, died of smallpox. Alfons Lemke, nine, and Michael Dormeier, fifteen, drowned in the Lün River. Any country boy can tell you a dozen stories like this.

Let me say also that Lothar and I had given ourselves plenty of opportunities to meet a similar fate; only recently had we grown beyond the age at which boys easily part with life simply out of stupidity or derring-do.

But today was different. We felt ourselves truly staring death in the face for the first time. And it stared back—giving us time to realize the inevitable, to appreciate the gravity of this moment, and to pass through every stage from false hope to acceptance of the inescapable. Our hour had come to settle accounts with this world, to come to grips with life's end. As our brief final moments flowed by, we had to assess how well we'd lived. After all, we would soon be held accountable.

I felt neither fear nor self-pity—only a silent resignation. The good Lord had seen fit to grant each of us only two decades of life, but by his grace, they were all good years. Lothar and I should be grateful.

In such moments, one's senses become particularly acute. Sounds and smells seized my awareness. I discerned and stared at distinct blades among the meadow grass, and separate bubbling water drops in the brook, and individual leaves on a yellowing larch nearby. People are right when they say the sun is brighter, the air sweeter, and life more beautiful just before you die.

Then all sorts of nonsense crept into my head. My imagination painted images of graves and funeral processions on Rundschau's streets. I could almost see fiery reflections, as if torch-bearing Canton Guards had come to burn the plague-ridden village along with all its inhabitants. In that orange glow, bodies lay on the ground with red-spotted cheeks and lumps on their throats. The bodies were people I knew well. Judge Holgert. Mama Bittner. The blacksmith Karl Reinecke. The carpenter Joachim Vogel. Father Theodor Riechmann, our parish priest.

And Lothar Lange.

Under the beech boughs, I turned to him beside me and thought, *What devilry could this be?*

Judging by his appearance, Lothar was also out of sorts. He sat frowning, leaning back against the tree's trunk.

Flashing suddenly in my mind was this: *Who'll get it first—him or me?* Ashamed of this unworthy thought, I silently asked the Lord for forgiveness. I, too, made the sign of the cross.

In that moment Lothar looked at me. His blue eyes grew dark. I sensed some daring plan brewing in his head.

"Waldheim—it's not far," he said slowly. The farm that Bertha Zellermann fled was in fact a two-hour walk through the woods up the side of Mount Tannenberg, and perhaps a half-day by the easier roundabout route, crossing mostly gentle slopes.

"Can you watch the sheep?" Lothar asked me.

I nodded in bewilderment.

Lothar squeezed my arm, jumped up, whistled for one of his dogs, then set out straight for the ancient pines covering Mount Tannenberg.

Over the many decades since then, my memory has returned often to the resolve I'd witnessed that moment in Lothar. It was of a special kind—the resolve of someone who, having won a battle with his inner self, moves to act quickly out of fear that should his doubts return, he might no longer have strength to overcome them.

Glimpsing Lothar's bold resolve was not enough—after he'd passed from my sight—to inspire my own better thoughts during the hours I was watching his sheep. My resignation deepened into grief, especially as I recalled the expectations for my life that I'd come to embrace—particularly in regard to Veronika Genscher, the weaver's daughter. Within just a couple of years—after I'd proven myself to be a real provider, able to support a household, according to the custom for such things in Rundschau—Veronika was to be my bride.

Not until evening approached, as the sun was ready to set behind the snow-covered ridge in the west, did Lothar finally return to the Kreuzbach waterfall. He drove before him a flock of sheep.

"Forty-seven head," he announced to me. He looked tired, but smiled. His arms were smeared to the elbows in something that looked like mud.

Lothar collapsed on the ground next to me. The filth on his arms, I realized, was sheep manure.

After catching his breath, he explained that he'd taken the long way back in returning from the farm at Waldheim.

Well, I told myself, *watch and learn, Arnold Enke, harness-maker's son: while you wallow in despair, your friend takes action like a man.*

The sheep he'd rescued had bunched themselves up into a solid mass, herded closely by Lothar's dog. They looked dirty and scraggly in comparison to our Rundschau flock. With darkness nearing, we needed to lead all these sheep into their night's keeping, but Lothar sat still. I saw tears in his eyes.

He explained more. He'd entered the Waldheim farm, opened the pens, and tended to the sheep, all the while trying not to look toward the houses with their corpses within. Two sheep, he discovered, were unable to walk. "I had no choice but to leave them there," he said sadly. "All the rest are here. To be honest, I thought it would be worse."

He stripped off his clothes and jumped into the brook to wash himself.

Could this autumn-cold water cleanse away not just the filth but also any infection Lothar might have caught at the farm? Was he crazy to risk his life by walking into the plague's den for the sake of some miserable sheep?

But Lothar was thinking bigger. Splashing out of the icy water to where his clothes lay, he called to me. "Maybe now Frau Bertha won't end up a penniless beggar—on top of her other misfortunes."

I reminded Lothar, however, that the villagers might be furious at his bringing among them these sheep coming straight from a plague-ravaged farm.

Lothar agreed. "It's too risky." But he had a plan. We would drive the Waldheim sheep this evening to an abandoned farm half a league from Rundschau. The following mornings, when Lothar drove his own flock from the village, he would make a detour to pick up Frau Bertha's sheep from their secret new home, then drop them off again on the way back. Later, he could disappear until nightfall, spending time with the hidden sheep to clean and comb their wool.

"Arnie," he declared solemnly, "this must be kept secret."

I agreed.

Chapter 3
A Simple Thing

THE NEXT DAY—Thursday, October second—passed in Rundschau as if it were a dream. Work wasn't done. Everyone sat in their homes and wouldn't set foot outside. Shutters stayed closed on many windows.

Everyone was waiting for someone to get sick.

No one did.

In the morning Lothar drove his sheep—including his extra flock—into the mountains. In the evening he drove them back home.

At dawn on the morning of October third, a surprise awaited us. For the first time in living memory, even among old-timers, the tolling of the parish church's bell summoned worshipers to mass not on Sunday, but Friday.

Under other circumstances, eight or ten people might have come to find out what was going on, then return to tell their neighbors. But the threat of plague was on every mind. The bell's ringing had hardly ceased when the church's huge main hall was filled.

My eyes searched the somber crowd and found Lothar Lange. Instead of driving out his sheep, he'd come to the church like everyone else. I was relieved that Lothar's appearance showed no hint of sickness.

Lothar saw me as well. "What's going on?" his eyes asked. I raised an eyebrow to answer: "We find out soon enough."

Farther across the crowd I spotted August Genscher the weaver, so grim-faced that it nearly startled me. Standing beside him, resting her head on his shoulder, was his daughter Veronika. Her expression held a solemn helplessness that was unutterably sweet to me.

I knew that no one here wondered if the bell had been rung by mistake. The faces around me were as sorrowfully anxious as I'd ever seen in this place. With the plague having devoured Waldheim, Rundschau's residents surely anticipated being called any moment before the Lord to answer for their sins. If the parish priest thought a Friday morning mass was a proper prelude for this—well, so be it.

As the last arriving villagers squeezed into the hushed congregation, my eyes went to where they often did on Sunday mornings here. First, to a large wooden statue of the Virgin Mary to the left of the altar, carved long ago by an unknown master. Our Lady stood clad in a dark blue mantle and white head covering, her head mournfully lowered, her hands folded on her breast. Over her hands the woodcarving master had placed her heart, enveloped in flames and enclosed in a crown of thorns. The crown was real—woven of real thorns, as a full-sized replica of the one that Roman soldiers had thrust upon the head of our Savior in the court of their Praetorium in Jerusalem.

I glanced next to my right—to a recess in the south wall that bore a fresco depicting the Passion of Christ. It had been painted before I was born, the gift of some eminent nobleman from far away who'd commissioned a German artist for this work. In my childhood years, if I became bored (gracious Lord, forgive me) during the sermon, my eye would examine this fresco, and over time I committed its features to memory. Even now, I can easily recall these details.

Under a scarlet sky, before whitewashed Jerusalem walls, a strange procession moves. In the picture's center is our thorn-crowned Savior bent beneath the weight of the cross. He's surrounded by a dense crowd in which one can discern every sort of modern person. In one spot, for example, is a pompous nobleman wearing a golden chain, a sable-collared velvet waistcoat, and a gaudily feathered beret. Nearby, a merchant sports on his belt a purse overflowing with gold coin. And there's a soldier—representing a Roman centurion apparently, but wearing the blackened steel armor of the Canton Guard, complete with rooster-plumed helmet, and hoisting a cruel-bladed halberd.

All their faces wear ugly sneers. Here in general, only the countenance of the Lord breathes peace and beauty; except for him, the entire procession is depicted as a parade of scowling freaks.

Ugliest of all is the face of the person in the fresco who always arrested my attention most: someone purple-robed, with a red three-cornered cap crowning a tonsure—a bishop! His visage is horribly contorted—a grimace instead of a face. This figure once appeared to me in a nightmare clouded by sulfur smell, and he suggested we take a trip to hell, where room had been reserved for sinners such as me.

A sound broke off my reflections upon the fresco; close by, the door of the sacristy opened, and out came our priest, Reverend Theodor Riechmann, accompanied by Deacon Andreas Vogt.

Father Theodor, short and nimble, was in his black cassock. Today, as often before, his wispy white hair reminded me of a dandelion's fluff.

As we all stood, his opening words were brief. "Today, my children, is Friday, the day of the Lord's Passion. Let us pray." He nodded to Deacon Vogt, turned to the altar, and started the mass.

"*In nomine Patris, et Filii, et Spiritus Sancti...*"

"Amen," we responded.

As the sacred words continued, I began thinking how good it was that Father Theodor had called us here two days ahead of schedule. Yesterday everyone had been paralyzed with fear— the village seemed dead already, before plague had touched a single soul here. It was terrible to imagine what could happen if this lethargic consternation lasted another day or two. We might have become an unmanageable herd, crazed with terror, but Father Theodor would not let this happen. Rundschau indeed had a shepherd, a good and firm shepherd who would not abandon his flock.

We listened to the Latin litany; we sang along where we could. I again looked at faces around me. The expressions were becoming more composed, more sober and sensible. Little by little, these villagers began looking human again— more like the face of Christ in the fresco.

The communion went by, and we sang. After the final blessing, while everyone waited for Father Theodor to dismiss us, he had another surprise. He closed the prayer book and fixed upon us his small, kind eyes.

"My children." He spoke in German. "I thank you for coming today to the call of the old bell. I ask you now to be seated and listen carefully; I want to give a sermon."

If he wants a sermon, so be it. We all sat down.

"Children," uttered Father Theodor. His voice made me feel like a child again; I was sure others around me felt the same—even the giant blacksmith, Karl Reinecke; even old Jürgen, Lothar Lange's foster father, old enough to be his grandfather. "Children, you see what is happening. In lands and countries all around, our brothers and sisters have been dying, while we in Rundschau thoughtlessly wasted the days allotted us by our good Lord. Now the calamity has arrived on our doorstep. Linden is struck down. Waldheim, whose residents were dear to many of us, is wiped out, along with those who fled there for sanctuary but brought death instead.

"We're surrounded on all sides. Perhaps tomorrow, perhaps

the next day, the fatal spark may flare up in our homes too."

His voice reverberated beneath the church's vaulted ceiling. "Nevertheless, my children, we must not lose heart. Hard times are sent to test the endurance of our faith. I rang the bell, and you came—which bears witness that faith indeed is still in your hearts. Nevertheless, for many of you, inner strength nears the point of exhaustion. So, what should we do?"

What should we do?—this was the question tormenting us all. Had God in his mercy revealed to Father Theodor a way out? A way out meant hope. Or at least a meaningful death, if no hope remained.

As the sermon paused, the church was so quiet, I could hear the faint crackle of candlewicks. I took a breath and looked around. From habit, I glanced again to the fresco, to the peaceful countenance of the Lord. A question returned that I'd contemplated for years: How was it possible to maintain such an inspired and detached look while carrying one's own cross to one's own execution, surrounded by such terrible grimaces?

Father Theodor continued. He was speaking in his usual manner: loudly, but sincerely and intimately. "I admit the plague has frightened me no less than you. I fully recognize —as you may—that if our sins were measured, they would outweigh the worst possible punishment, and many times over. God, however, does not desire the sinner's death, but rather wishes him to repent and live.

"Although we cannot discover how many more days the Lord has measured out for our lives, it is in our power to prove our repentance. Repentance is our mightiest weapon against the devil, who has been allowed to harm Christian folk with plagues and all possible misfortunes. Cities and kingdoms crash and fall before him. Death marches through the world like a victorious army of the evil one. Is there anything that might halt this onslaught?"

Again he paused at length. Again my eye went to the fresco. Years ago, when I'd grown up a bit, Father Riechmann explained to me this painting's secret meaning. At Golgotha the Savior was followed by every human sin—including pride (the nobleman), greed (the merchant), and manslaughter (the soldier). And as for that hideous bishop— well, the most horrible sin of all was that of the Pharisees: their profanation of the Holy Spirit, when they accused our blessed Savior of deadly sins, declaring his power to be from Beelzebub, for which they condemned him to death. And the leading Pharisee was Caiaphas—who was, as it were, Jerusalem's bishop. It was he who was depicted by the brush of the German master.

Father Theodor's voice deepened. "As this plague advances, can anything—anything whatsoever—be done?

"My children, all day Wednesday I splattered the floor of my cell with tears and beseeched our merciful Lord with my question. That night, in the darkest hours, it dawned on me. And I could hardly believe it myself—how could I have missed such a simple answer?"

He raised his hand. He held a small gilded crucifix.

"The cross!" he said, his voice ringing out. "The gospel's power! Our weapon of victory over death, our hope of redemption, our gateway to resurrection and eternal life!

"This moment when Satan seems triumphant, when the sheep of Christ's flock fall by thousands into his open jaws— what would vex our enemy most, and bring joy to our merciful Savior at the same time? Praising the holy and living cross!

"My children, the devil in his pride considers this world his own, subject to his power. But it has been saved on the cross by our Redeemer—our Lord who is forever the King! Therefore our duty is to never lose heart over hell's apparent triumph, but to resolutely proclaim the Lord's victory, as is fitting for Christ's warriors and knights.

"You and I are simple sinners, but within our souls—by

the grace of God—abides love for Jesus Christ, who died for our sins on the cross. This love gives us ultimate joy, even in our worst affliction. In sickness, in torment, in temptation, if you and I will keep our love for Christ and for each other, and preserve a joyful spirit—then through us, the Lord is victorious and the devil overcome. This is the mystery of the cross."

Yet once more, Father Theodor paused. All around me, people sat eagerly erect. What was coming next?

"When I remembered all this," he continued, "my soul was filled with such jubilation that I ran to Deacon Andreas to share with him my revelation. We prayed together, considering what we must do. In such a dark time for our little village, how could we glorify the redeeming cross of Christ? We sat and talked about the Passion of the Lord, and we wept.

"And then I, my children—surprising even myself—made a suggestion to Deacon Andreas. What if all of us together were to actually resurrect the events of the Passion of our blessed Jesus Christ—in real life, so to speak? We thought this over—and decided to put it to your judgment. Here's what we propose."

Father Theodor caught his breath. We were all ears; something unheard of, it seemed, was about to unfold.

"Together you and I—the residents of the village of Rundschau, District of Rundschau, Canton of Schwarzwald—right here, in the streets of our village, shall present and reenact the sacred events described in the Gospels of the Passion of our Savior."

Solemnly, he went on: "With God's help, we shall bring before his eyes—and the eyes of all good people—the divine act called the Mysteria, which we will dedicate to the glory of our crucified Lord! This is how we'll defeat the evil one!"

For a moment, silence reigned under the church's vault.

Then everyone started speaking at once.

Chapter 4
This Pressing Question

I MUST HAND IT to Father Theodor Riechmann. As outlandish as his idea was, it was already proving a stroke of genius for the mending of our community. The people of Rundschau, who just an hour earlier had filed into the church as if for their own funeral, were now transformed.

Around me in the congregation, I heard expressions of excitement from every direction, as if a crowd of children had just been told they were going to the fair. How amazing this seemed to me! The danger was still present; the plague lurked silently in our homes, ready to show itself; but our fears had melted away. No longer were we simply waiting to die; we were part of something new and fascinating, a divine act—the Mysteria.

What an amazing creature man is! One moment he may seem utterly crushed by misfortunes; then suddenly he sees a truly worthy meaning and purpose to them, and he's ready to stand beside you shoulder to shoulder, steadfastly facing whatever else life throws your way.

But what, exactly, was this Mysteria supposed to look like? Big Reinecke the blacksmith was first to call out this question that morning in the church, as he ran his fingers through his red beard. He wasn't alone in wondering about this. Of course, at one time or another, most of us had traveled to Linden or elsewhere for holidays and seen there what was called a passion play. And one Christmas, Lothar and I happened to witness a performance which a Linden street-banner announced as a "Great and Amazing Presentation in Five Acts with Prologue and Intermission about the Birth of Christ, the Adoration of the Magi, and Herod's Massacre of the 14,000

Infants in Judean Bethlehem." It was a puppet show—but this was not, I gathered, what Father Theodor had in mind.

As the noise of the crowd died away, our priest stepped down from the pulpit to further explain. We would simply enact from the Gospels, line by line, the holy Passion of our Lord—and do it right outside our doors in Rundschau. This way we would glorify the Lord not only with our voices, as happens when one simply reads the Gospels aloud, but with our whole bodies and even with the streets of our village! Father Riechmann also added that the mass that we just had was in a way reenacting the Lord's Supper, and that during this reenactment a mystery of sacrament (called *Mysteria* in Latin) takes place.

He also said we must do this as soon as possible. "Time is short, my children. Our lives hang by a thread, and any of us could be struck ill any moment."

This reminder in no way dampened our excitement. Rather, prominent voices in the congregation called out ideas and suggestions that were eagerly affirmed by other voices, and the Mysteria began taking on a practical shape in our minds.

It was decided that our procession for the Mysteria would begin at the house of Stolz the woodcutter—our village's first house on the main road coming from Linden. The procession would then move up our main street—which climbed a slope—and end on the main square in front of the church and town hall. This plan was heartily commended by Judge Holgert, who'd learned so much during his studies in Bologna, and who pointed out that the path in Jerusalem along which Christ carried his cross went uphill for the most part. So too would our procession.

It was also decided that we would construct two wooden platforms. The first, in front of the Stolz house at the procession's beginning, would represent the Praetorium of Pontius

Pilate and his Roman soldiers; a scourging post would be added nearby. The second platform would rise on the main square to represent Golgotha; there the cross would be planted.

Such an undertaking was complex, but everyone agreed that a week was a suitable amount of time to prepare.

"Next Friday then," announced Father Theodor, "a week from today—God willing—we'll perform our Mysteria."

Three marshals were chosen and put in charge of various aspects of the preparations. Deacon Andreas Vogt, being highly esteemed and literate, would coach and direct the actors, and also oversee the entire production. August Genscher the weaver volunteered to come up with costumes, shrouds, sashes, soldier standards, and whatever additional decoration was necessary.

The third marshal was my father, Hans-Heinrich Enke the harness-maker. He would be responsible for the necessary props such as weapons for the legionaries, Pilate's wash basin, and so forth.

The congregation's interest grew even keener as the moment came to begin assigning roles. With so many wanting to take part in the Mysteria, and with the number of speaking roles rather limited, this selection process might have become quite disorderly. Father Theodor, however, calmed everyone down with a reminder that the majority of us must be content with the honor of being spectators. But crowd scenes were required where a great many could participate, and moreover, everyone's fullest efforts would be needed in the week-long preparations.

Now—who would take the major roles?

As before, respected voices in the congregation offered suggestions that were quickly met with favor. Judge Holgert was a natural fit for the role of Pontius Pilate, the procurator of Judea. Genscher the weaver and Fleische the innkeeper showed humble deference in being willing to portray two major culprits in our Savior's death: the high priests Caiaphas and Annas. Young Paul Hofbauer, who was Fleische the innkeeper's servant, would play John, the Lord's beloved disciple.

Margreta Bern was chosen to play Mary Magdalene. For the role of Mary the mother of Jesus, we chose young Anna-Maria Schubert, the fiancée of Anton Stolz the woodcutter; her face was marked by quiet beauty and beautiful brown eyes.

Nervously, I myself called out a suggestion: that Veronika, the daughter of Genscher the weaver, be given the role of saintly Veronica—to be the one so moved with pity upon seeing Jesus carry his cross that she would offer him her veil to wipe his forehead. To my relief and gladness, this choice was met with immediate approval from the congregation, and with a blush on my bride-to-be's face.

Then it fell to me and to young Klaus Zillendorf to be selected as Roman legionaries.

All this went smoothly. But the most prominent role remained unfilled, though this pressing question was doubtless on everyone's mind. It was uttered aloud by the innkeeper, Eberhard Fleische: "Who will play the Savior himself, our Lord Christ?"

A moment earlier the church had been filled with lively conversation; now a baffled silence fell over the congregation. People looked at each other. Who would take it upon himself to portray the One who is both Lamb of God and Shepherd of our souls—to be sentenced and scourged in the Praetorium, to walk the way of the cross, to be crucified on Golgotha?

No one, of course, was about to nominate himself; we in Rundschau were not so presumptuous.

The silence deepened. Truly, there was no one worthy.

It was at this moment I realized how deeply serious—even terrifying—our undertaking was going to be. Those around me must have sensed this also.

Suddenly the right choice dawned on me. Of course! I should have realized it at once. After a deep breath, I opened my mouth to speak up again—when Reinecke the blacksmith beat me to the punch. Stroking his red beard, he spoke loudly the very name that was about to roll off my tongue.

"Lothar Lange."

The sound of voices again filled the church, expressing approval. Reinecke had hit the nail on the head.

I looked across the crowd toward Lothar. He wore the same stunned expression I'd seen while telling him the fate of Waldheim farm. He looked back and forth from Father Theodor to Reinecke the blacksmith, as if hoping one or both would quickly think better of this horrible idea, and reject it.

Instead, Father Theodor nodded and smiled at my friend. "Why not, Lothar?" he called out. "After all, you too are a shepherd!"

Chapter 5
Lothar

MUCH LATER—a year or so after the events of the Mysteria, which I'll soon describe—I discovered something strange.

In those later days when Lothar was no longer around, I noticed how people's memories of him started changing—to the point that little was left of the real person who'd actually lived among us. In these transformed memories, Lothar wasn't Lothar at all, but rather like some sort of angel who descended from heaven into Rundschau.

There's no doubt how all this started—it was Frau Margreta Bern and the other village matrons in their busy-body chatter among themselves. It was enough to make you sick: "Oh, he was so wonderful," they would say. "So sweet." "Such a good boy." "Always so open to my advice." They made it sound as if Lothar Lange's greatest virtue was being always affectionate and obliging toward themselves. "*Our* Lothar," they called him.

Gradually they slipped into ridiculous babbling that made your ears burn with embarrassment. "Ah, our Lothar had those cute sapphire eyes." As if they were cooing over a baby!

And of course, because Lothar was a saint, then so were they, since they understood him so well and faithfully guarded his memory.

I'm absolutely certain Lothar would have been disgusted by such talk on his account. (Who in their right mind wouldn't be?)

I, however, knew the real Lothar; this is the person I'll faithfully describe to you now. My witnesses are Father Theodor Riechmann, and old man Jürgen Zielmeister, and many others who are no longer with us. When the time comes for the angel

Gabriel to blow his horn, these men will rise up and testify that Arnold Enke, son of a harness-maker from Rundschau, is telling no lies upon these pages.

Lothar was a month and a day older than I. His only sibling, his younger sister Martha, died as an infant, and when Lothar turned seven, both his parents also passed away. Because they were kind people who left behind such good memories of themselves, the entire village of Rundschau took upon itself the care and upbringing of orphaned Lothar. By decision of the village council, Lothar was placed with Jürgen Zielmeister the shepherd as his apprentice. Jürgen was growing old, and he'd already been thinking about finding his replacement.

Meanwhile young Lothar was welcome at every door. He fit in everywhere—especially at the house of my father, Hans-Heinrich Enke, who'd been quite close to Lothar's father, Dietrich Lange. Lothar and I became fast friends, and by age eight we were inseparable.

Lothar was always tall for his age. He grew to be agile and quick, with broad shoulders and a strong back, the kind one gets in our part of the world from hard work. His hair, which he parted down the middle, was dark brown and wavy. His complexion was smooth and unblemished, never marred by smallpox, which had ravaged the cheeks and foreheads of so many village children.

What distinguished Lothar most were his eyes, which were light gray when he first went to live with old man Jürgen, but within a year had changed to bright blue. Lothar and I believed that this was because of his work as a shepherd. He was helping his foster father from spring to fall in Alpine meadows, where he loved to gaze into our magnificent mountain sky, which is indeed a gift from God. Thanks to its location and altitude, Rundschau is more open than many places to the interplay of sun and sky. Even in winter we can get a good tan. Lothar was naturally pale and did not tan easily—so it was his eyes, not his skin, that changed color.

Those eyes and their mountain-sky blueness seemed closely connected to Lothar's distinctive inner qualities, which gave him an aura of purity—that's the best way I can describe it. He gave the impression of being a youth who was pure in heart and mind. This tended to make people enjoy his company.

Among Lothar's peers (like me), there were of course those who tried to be as pure as good Christian children should be. But whereas we tried, Lothar simply was. Meanwhile he lived side by side with us, played with us—tag, wrestling, ball games—and confided his youthful secrets to us, as we in turn did to him. He was there when we told scary stories in a dark barn. In so many ways he was normal— except a bit more natural than the rest of us, with a heart more pure, a soul more open. But then, my judgment may be biased.

Lothar seemed unaware of the unique impression he made upon people around him. Nevertheless, when he was no longer a child, this impression grew only stronger. Lothar was truly a favorite in the village, this humble, clear-hearted young shepherd whom everyone respected—which, I trust you understand, is quite different from being everyone's pal or chum.

For example, Lothar rarely took part in the banter and teasing that marked most village children's interactions. Of course, once you got him going, he could dish it out as well as the next guy, and get the better of some wisecracking big-mouth. But it seemed to give him no real pleasure, and the older he got, the more he avoided this sort of thing.

Growing older also meant that in the winter, when there was nothing better to do, he would join us boys in going off to neighboring villages—Lüneberg, Waltzholm, sometimes even Linden—to fight other gangs like our own. More than once Lothar came home with a badge of honor in the form of a black eye or bloodied nose. But around the age of fifteen, he began to lose interest in these forays. What he liked better was to trek into the mountains.

I often accompanied him. We would shoulder our skis and race up snow-covered fields, so that steam rose from our sweat-soaked clothing. Here by the still unfrozen waterfall at Kreuzbach, we cast off our clothes and plunged naked into the icy water. Then we ran and rolled in snowbanks until our bodies felt almost burning in the frigid Alpine air.

After putting our clothes back on, we put on our skis and flew like the wind down the slopes, dodging trees. We could easily have broken our necks in this game—but a different fate awaited us.

Meanwhile it became increasingly obvious over the years that Lothar had a God-given talent for shepherding. By age fifteen, he was taking out the sizeable village herd entirely on his own, and earning enough to support both himself and old man Jürgen Zielmeister, who now gave up this occupation and planted himself by his fireplace, carving dishware out of wood, and thanking God for blessing him in his old age with such a wonderful son. Jürgen also taught Lothar his wood-carving hobby, and in winter, when the sheep-tending was over, they both put their whittling knives to work. In the spring they rented a cart from Deacon Vogt, loaded it with wooden spoons, mugs, plates, and saucers, and took these to market at Linden. Their wares would quickly sell out.

As Lothar reached his late teens, my father and I helped him fix up old man Zielmeister's aging dwelling, making it worthy of some future household. So it was that Lothar stood firmly on his own two feet, and the whole village was guessing when and whom he would marry. Plenty of our village matrons with eligible daughters could easily imagine him as their choice for a groom. I suppose none of them ever thought that a man might have a different calling in this world than starting a family. Whatever the case may be, Lothar never paid attention to their schemes, and at the age of twenty he was still a virgin—his body as pure as his mind and heart.

Chapter 6
But a Pitiful Sinner

IN THE CHURCH that Friday morning of October third, when Lothar Lange realized that Reinecke the blacksmith would not withdraw his nomination of Lothar to perform the role of Christ, and that Father Theodor would not disapprove of this choice, Lothar himself leaped up to speak.

He insisted he was unsuitable, that he did not measure up to such a high honor. "Besides, I'm far too young. Everyone knows our Savior was thirty-three at the time of his Passion."

He was wringing his shepherd's cap in his hand. His voice intensified. "But most important, this performance is about portraying the Son of God who was free of sin, while I, Lothar Lange, am but a pitiful sinner with neither the audacity nor the ability to take this role."

Well, on one hand, he was quite right. But there was no other suitable candidate in all of Rundschau that day.

Besides, I didn't think any objection from Lothar could really have mattered. I was gaining an awareness that in those days in Rundschau, everything was unfolding as if guided by divine providence. As the Lord desired, so it was coming to pass.

Father Theodor had been watching Lothar attentively, his gaze growing ever warmer. "Without a doubt, you're correct, my child," he said, when Lothar finally ran out of words. "And I will add this: there's no man righteous enough in the whole world to be even the least bit worthy to take on the role of our Lord Jesus Christ. I'm happy, Lothar, that you realize this, for it increases your penitence.

"All the same, don't be afraid of this task. Everything in our

Mysteria will be a symbol as well as a sacrament. Everyone who participates will be helping to symbolize the fuller truth of our Lord's own Passion, so that all who see us will praise the glorious deed of the Savior. Therefore, while we understand your reluctance, we nevertheless beseech you to stay humble and accept this role, for it is crucial for the Mysteria."

After this explanation, Lothar said nothing more. But seeing his continued agitation, I decided that when we left the church, I must go and speak with him before he took his flock out to pasture.

All seemed in order for the Mysteria; Father Theodor gave us final words of exhortation for the coming week. "I warn you: we're undertaking a most serious endeavor—perhaps the most serious in our lives. We must pray most fervently that God Almighty allow us to see it through to the end. Meanwhile I urge you to refrain from sin and strengthen your devotion in every possible way." He dismissed us, and we began leaving the church.

We had lost all sense of time inside; midday was already past.

Beside the big pond next to the church stood Konrad Eisenstein, our village idler and good-for-nothing. He was entertaining himself by spitting into the pond. "Well, well," he called out to those of us passing by. "So you've decided to have some fun! A little celebration—your very last party, people of Rundschau, ha-ha!" Konrad's laughter was like the cawing of a crow.

His words were annoying, but nothing more. Who among us would pay heed to anything said by Konrad Eisenstein? He had turned up in Rundschau twenty years earlier (no one knew where from), and in all these years seemed never to change or even to age. He would sometimes cut wood or hunt or do odd jobs among us, then disappear for prolonged periods before returning. If anything was missing from a

Rundschau house or barn—say, a new horse-collar, or a skein of yarn left out to dry—everyone assumed the thief was Eisenstein, though he was never caught. In spite of his irregular work-life, Konrad seemed to want for nothing; he spent his evenings in Fleische's tavern sipping beer and snacking on duck legs, then slept in a shack on the edge of the village.

I rushed past Konrad and went to the house of Jürgen Zielmeister and Lothar. Inside, I was glad to see my friend hadn't yet hurried away to tend the sheep. But his reason for delay appeared strange.

"Lothar, what are you doing?"

Old Jürgen had brought out a hemp belt about a cubit wide. Lothar, bare-chested, stood holding it.

"Strengthening my devotion," he soberly answered, echoing Father Theodor's words. Lothar was going to wear this thing under his shirt for the purpose of mortifying his flesh.

At my request, he first allowed me to try it on. The brittle old fibers bristled, stinging mercilessly the naked skin of my back and belly.

I pulled it off and thrust it back to him. "Genuine torture," I acknowledged.

Lothar strapped it on, then stiffly donned his shirt on top of it. The hemp belt's abrasiveness at first brought tears to his eyes, but otherwise he did not betray his suffering with even a single twitch. "I will think of how our Jesus was scourged for our sins," he told me. "In comparison, wearing a hemp belt is nothing." He vowed he would not take it off until after the Mysteria.

We had no time to talk further. Lothar hurried away to his work with the sheep. I knew he would spend the rest of this day deep in thought.

Chapter 7
That Which Must Happen

THE NEXT DAY—Saturday, October fourth—Father Theodor and Deacon Andreas gathered a group of volunteers (including my father) and headed out for the Waldheim farm. They were to perform a burial service for Zellermann the hunter, his sons, and all the rest of the plague victims there. They planned to burn all the buildings along with the bodies therein.

Later in the day I was on an errand near the town square and saw them returning. As it happened, Konrad Eisenstein also was nearby, and he saw them too. "Well, boys," he shouted, "did you enjoy the plague aroma in the air? We'll smell it here in Rundschau before too long!"

My father glared at him; Konrad sauntered off giggling.

That evening at home, my father commented pensively to my mother and me: "I don't understand. All the property in Waldheim looked undisturbed—but the sheep were gone. Why would thieves take only the sheep?"

I quietly shook my head.

My mother then told us that Frau Bertha Zellermann was still lying with a fever at the house of Granny Krause the midwife. It wasn't the plague, but rather the result of a nervous breakdown that followed the terrible shock she'd experienced at Waldheim.

On Sunday after mass, Father Theodor and Deacon Andreas climbed in the deacon's cart and went off to make the rounds of farms and villages in the parish, to see how everyone was faring. When the two returned, they reported only one other place—Achendorf—where there was plague. But that was bad enough; at any moment the epidemic could rampage throughout the district.

Father Theodor said also that he'd mentioned far and wide our undertaking of the Mysteria in Rundschau. This news aroused interest in a few places, but indifferent silence in most others. Fear of plague was like a dark cloud everywhere, sapping people's strength and destroying their will. Dispersing that cloud was no easy task.

On Monday, the sixth of October, preparations for the Mysteria got underway in earnest. The mood I sensed among the people astounded me: elation and inspiration combined with diligent concentration on our common purpose. There was also a hint of resignation. What was missing was any sense of oppressive fear—despite our knowing, as before, that while we were alive and well today, everything could change tomorrow.

Hammers sounded in the town square where the Golgotha platform was being erected. Nearby, inside the church, Deacon Andreas addressed the gathered participants. He explained the order and meaning of everything our Mysteria would portray. He also read passages from the Gospels, while urging us to imagine ourselves being actually present there in Jerusalem when those great events unfolded for the redemption of the human race.

That evening, Lothar—having returned from his day's work with the sheep—asked me to join him at Deacon Vogt's house, where the two of them would go over the role of Christ for the first time. There, sitting rigidly (because of the hemp belt, I knew), Lothar astonished the deacon with a request. He wanted to use a real crown of thorns for the Mysteria—the very one that crowned the heart of Mary on her statue in the church.

"Lothar, my boy, what could make you wish for such a thing? That crown's made of blackthorn—horrible stuff, the thorns so long and sharp! They'll cut your head even if you wear a felt cap underneath."

Lothar said he needed no cap and didn't care if his head got scratched by a few thorns.

The deacon was bewildered. "But why?" I shared his puzzlement, especially knowing that my father, in his duties for the Mysteria, was already plaiting for Lothar a "symbolic" thorn-crown out of willow branches and pieces of tin.

Lothar explained. "I know the nails won't be real, nor the whip. But I want to try, even if just a little, to share in the experience of what our Savior felt in those moments."

Deacon Vogt promised he would discuss this with Father Riechmann.

Early the next day, the deacon was at my father's door to cancel the plans for the willow-and-tin crown. Father Theodor, it seemed, had concluded there was nothing sacrilegious or prideful in Lothar's wish for a crown of real thorns, and had given this request his blessing.

As the Mysteria participants gathered again on Tuesday and Wednesday morning for further instruction and training from Deacon Andreas, I battled a deepening concern. The closer we came to the Mysteria, the less I liked my role as a Roman legionary. The easy part was standing guard at Pilate's palace and later at the crucifixion site. But I would also have to participate in "scourging" Lothar and in placing the crown of thorns on his head. I was to treat him roughly while escorting him to Golgotha. And in conclusion, it was I who would "nail" him to the cross, using leather straps my father had made, which I would tie around Lothar's wrists and ankles. Since Lothar was playing the role of Christ, all this made me none other than the crucifier of the Savior of the human race. Think whatever you like, but this growing realization sickened me.

Making me feel worse was Deacon Andreas's further instruction personally to me: "Keep true to the events."

He then went on to expand my soldier's role. As my

suffering victim revealed his thirst in a cry from the cross, I would be the one holding up to him a vinegar-soaked sponge on the end of my spear. And once this victim died—it was I who would take that spear and "pierce" Lothar's side.

Well—I was near the point of quitting my role in the Mysteria.

I openly confessed all this to Lothar that afternoon, after going out to the mountain meadows to find him. "How can I bring myself to do this?" I lamented. "Even symbolically! How can I do to *you* what those barbarians did to our good Lord?"

Lothar sighed. After a silent moment he said, "Your doing it is still better for me. It will all be easier if I have an old friend at my side." He cast his blue eyes on me and smiled. "Even if he appears to be straight out of a Roman legion."

More at ease now, we sat by a spring to pray together and eat. Lothar brought out cheese. I had only bread, since I was limiting myself to bread and water for the duration of the week, as prompted by Father Theodor's admonition to strengthen our devotion. In fact, almost all the villagers took one vow or another.

Lothar's eyes looked weary. I knew that each night, after spending time going over his Christ role with Deacon Vogt, Lothar would run a half-league in darkness to the old farm where he was keeping the Waldheim sheep. Lighting a lamp, he set about further tending them: combing out tangled wool, salving their sores, and calming them with his voice. He also made sure all their coats were color-marked with the Waldheim marking. Once he finally arrived home to rest, he had to continue enduring the hemp belt but also—I was certain—his anxious anticipation of what awaited him on Friday.

"How are you holding up?" I asked.

He answered with a tired grin and a sigh.

After washing down my bread with water from the

spring, I informed Lothar of the progress Klaus Zillendorf and I had made in getting outfitted as Roman legionaries. In my father's trunk I'd found my grandfather's chain mail wrapped in greased rags. It fit me surprisingly well. My father also brought out a leather shoulder-belt and his old leather cap with a feather. I put these on also, to the admiration of my father and little brother Thomas. Then I went down to the village pond to see my reflection in the water. It was definitely a soldier's look, I told Lothar—the proper incarnation of the sin of manslaughter.

Meanwhile my co-legionary Klaus Zillendorf had arranged with the innkeeper Eberhard Fleische to borrow chain mail and an old iron helmet, which normally hung over the hearth in the inn's main hall. "In exchange," I reported to Lothar, "Klaus has to chop a week's worth of firewood for Herr Fleische."

Klaus also borrowed the innkeeper's biggest carving knife, which looked monstrous enough to serve as his Roman short sword, his *gladius*. "And for this he'll haul fifteen buckets of water to Herr Fleische's kitchen."

I stretched my legs. "But as for me—now I have to find a spear." I hadn't found anything suitable. Rundschau men had numerous military and hunting spears, but they were too long, too heavy, too sharp. We needed a fake spear for our Mysteria.

"How about my staff?" Lothar asked. He passed it to me.

It seemed the right weight and length. And very straight.

"Sharpen the top a little here," Lothar said, "and it easily looks like a spear. I can get myself a new staff in the forest."

I felt uneasy about this. For one thing, was it right that the staff with which a shepherd herded his flock should become a soldier's spear to pierce the sacred heart of Jesus?

I said to Lothar, "But for you to find a young tree this straight for another staff—that could be tough."

Lothar nodded.

I extended his staff toward him. "I can go to Vogel the carpenter for some sort of pole for the spear."

"No, Arnie." Lothar gently pushed the staff back to me. "We both know Herr Vogel is fully absorbed in working on the cross."

Indeed, I preferred not to bother the carpenter—not only because of the cross, but also in light of his responsibilities for managing the construction of the two platforms at each end of our main street. So I accepted Lothar's offer.

He asked me, "And how goes Herr Vogel's work on the cross? Did I tell you he came and took my measurements, to make sure the thing will be long enough and broad enough?"

I hadn't heard this. In an eerie way, it seemed like measuring a corpse for a casket.

"Well," I answered, "it was slow work for Herr Vogel at first. He wanted cypress wood, but there's none to be had in Rundschau. Then he settled on beechwood, which he said would be strong enough and easy to work with. He took beams that were meant for an addition to Fleische's inn—four of them, which Herr Fleische at first found himself reluctant to part with, or so I hear." This had been reported to me by Fleische's servant Paul Hofbauer, who was to portray the apostle John in our Mysteria.

"But then," I continued, "the first two beams Herr Vogel tried were warped somehow, and he couldn't make them fit together properly. So last evening he put down his saw and plane, shut himself up in his house, and spent all night in prayer, kneeling before the crucifix, bowing his forehead to the floor. So I was told. And today people were saying his work goes well. He hopes to have the cross finished by nightfall. It should be quite something to see."

Lothar agreed. "Herr Vogel is an expert carpenter. And careful. He told me this cross will have a perch for my feet.

He says that without it—if all my weight hung only by my hands—I'd soon wrench out my shoulders and tear tendons. Not to mention the suffocating pressure on my chest."

I hoped Herr Vogel truly knew what he was doing. "Lothar—perhaps tonight we should go by Herr Vogel's workshop and examine it."

Lothar was quiet. Then he nodded.

That evening, before he returned to Deacon Vogt's to further prepare for his role on Friday, Lothar and I briefly visited Joachim Vogel's brightly lit workshop. It was filled with our fellow villagers surrounding the cross, which lay on braces in the middle of the shop. Several people praised its craftsmanship.

Lothar seemed hardly to notice everyone as he stared at the cross. I stood beside him.

There was indeed something fascinating about its appearance. The lightly colored beechwood seemed to glow.

Near the base of the cross was the special perch Vogel had made, looking solid and firmly attached. Here Lothar could place his feet—when that which must happen would happen.

On a workbench nearby lay a sign with the Latin inscription *Iesus Nasoreus Rex Iudaeorum*—Jesus of Nazareth, King of the Jews. This would be nailed over Lothar's head.

And I was the one who must nail it.

Chapter 8
Final Hours

AS LOTHAR AND I slipped out of the crowded carpenter's shop that night, we heard someone speaking of a miracle that apparently had occurred in Rundschau shortly before Lothar and I returned from the meadows.

We both went to Deacon Vogt's—Lothar had once more asked that I join him for his evening session—and there we learned the details of today's miracle.

The background to it was that Helmut Vogt, the deacon's son, had made the rounds of Rundschau houses yesterday collecting donations for Mysteria expenses. Earlier this morning, Karl Reinecke the blacksmith received these collected funds and added his own money to it. Then he hitched his chestnut horse to his wagon and set out for Linden.

Earlier this evening he'd returned. In the wagon—holding bagpipes, fiddles, flutes, and drums—sat a group of seven musicians.

How on earth did Reinecke the blacksmith manage to find musicians in plague-stricken Linden and convince them to come to Rundschau? How had he made his way through the cordon of Canton Guards? What did he tell their commanding officer (who must have thought Rundschau residents had lost their minds)? These were questions Deacon Andreas couldn't answer. But the miracle happened, and it meant that our Mysteria would be accompanied by musical instruments, something truly wonderful.

I learned a further detail about this at home later that evening, after my brother Thomas had been sent to bed. My father stood at our hearth and watched the blaze before him. Karl Reinecke had spoken to him after his return from Linden, and the sturdy blacksmith appeared shaken. He told my father how an old woman in Linden had rushed up to him while he was negotiating with the musicians. She started howling: "A funeral feast! You're buying your funeral feast, blacksmith Reinecke! There'll soon be such a feast for *you!*"

Reinecke said he gripped the sideboard of his wagon and responded, "Woman, don't push me."

She moved on, but for a long time he heard her howling down the street: "A funeral feast! A funeral feast! A funeral feast in Rundschau!" This voice kept ringing in Reinecke's thoughts on the long drive home.

"Have a talk with the priest," my father had counseled him.

My father looked now at me. "Karl is convinced there's something satanic at work in this."

I couldn't disagree.

My father gazed back into the fire. "But the Lord also works. Not a single one of us in Rundschau has fallen sick, although Karl tells me Linden suffers so greatly, and whole regions elsewhere are wiped out. But here..." He rested a hand on the mantle, then turned again to me. "Even Bertha Zellermann is recovering from her fever, getting slowly onto her feet. So I'm told."

Yes, here in Rundschau, we had been granted a stay of execution—and who could doubt that this was for the Mysteria's sake? The Lord our God was looking favorably upon the offering we had prepared.

The next morning—Thursday the ninth—the sound of pounding hammers resumed on the village's main street, where the two platforms neared completion. At the Golgotha platform in the square, I saw Joachim Vogel bent over in focused labor. He was making a special socket there to hold his cross erect.

At a long table set up temporarily near the church, I saw Genscher the weaver (and his daughter Veronika) with a crowd of women, who had brought out sewn banners and shrouds and various linen outfits, which Genscher and Veronika were inspecting.

As I ran errands later that afternoon, my path took me by old Jürgen Zielmeister's house. He stood in the doorway with his hand on his foster son's shoulder. Lothar must have come in earlier than usual from the mountains—perhaps to receive more instruction from the deacon.

I heard the old shepherd's booming voice: "Don't worry, boy; you've never once let old Jürgen down. I'll not let you down either." He stepped inside.

Lothar saw me then, and came alongside me, with his three dogs at his heels. "I asked him to take care of my sheep tomorrow," he explained. I could see this had been an uncomfortable request. To Lothar, Jürgen Zielmeister had become a true father to be cherished and cared for, and who was no longer suited for strenuous outdoor labor.

"He's honored that you asked," I assured my friend. "And he'll do fine. This will be his contribution to our Mysteria."

As we walked together along the street, out of nowhere appeared Konrad Eisenstein. "Hey, Lothar," he shouted. "I suppose you're counting down your final hours! By this time tomorrow, you'll be dangling on high—in front of all the good folk of Rundschau!"

He was as despicable as ever. He clasped his hands, shook his head, and spoke with mock grief: "Throwing away your youth! And for what? Do you even know?" He stepped closer as his voice deepened. "Aren't you a bit young to be putting on Christ's shoes? God will make you pay for this! And don't you wonder how?"

Lothar and I stopped walking. Lothar's face reddened with fury. His eyes darkened; they seemed to shoot out sparks of dark blue. The three dogs, ears erect, stared at Konrad, who kept taunting.

"Poor Lothar! Poor guy! You never groped that wench behind the barn, never had that roll in the hay! Better hop to it, brother, or it'll be too late to get some sugar!"

Lothar looked bewildered. He glanced my way and whispered, "What wench?"

I could hold my tongue no longer. "Listen, Konrad Eisenstein! You were going somewhere, right? Well, get going!"

Konrad turned as if he'd just noticed me. "And then there's Arnie," he proclaimed. "How are you, Arnie? Tomorrow you hang your best friend out to dry—not bad, eh? Yeah, that's life, boy—get used to it."

"I'll jump him," I told Lothar from the corner of my mouth. I wanted to pummel Konrad's smirking face.

"No," answered Lothar, having already regained his composure. "Don't bother. This is no time to raise your hand against anyone. Even Eisenstein."

Sometimes he was capable of showing remarkable restraint, Lothar Lange was.

Konrad threw up his hands as if to say, "I've lost interest." He rambled off. Before he disappeared, he turned and yelled: "Lothar, my friend, remember the Scriptures: Cursed is he who hangs on a tree!"

His cawing laughter startled a flock of sparrows. Lothar's dogs barked angrily.

Chapter 9
What Is Truth?

FRIDAY, OCTOBER TENTH—dawn was breaking on the day of our Mysteria.

At the summons of the church bell, residents of Rundschau made their way through the streets, past buildings and fences decorated in garlands, colored ribbons, banners, and patterned fabrics.

Inside the church, everyone assembled for a celebration of mass. At Father Theodor's request, all the performers attended in costume.

I found Lothar standing by the south wall, just beneath the fresco. He wore a white robe, his face pale and concentrated. He told me he'd been awake all night.

"In your place," I told him, "I couldn't have slept either."

I was wearing my chain mail and leather shoulder-strap, and held upright my Roman "spear." Under my arm I carried my leather cap with its feather.

After our celebration of mass together, we stepped out. The hour for our Mysteria had come.

The day had begun sunny, but now dense gray clouds moved in. Cold air gusted from the mountains. Lothar shivered in his robe, having only a thin shirt beneath it. The hemp belt had at last been shed.

Singing *Veni, Sancte Spiritus*—"Come, Holy Spirit"—the assembly headed downhill toward the finished platform standing in front of Anton Stolz's house. Within the thickening crowd on our main street were a great many visitors from other villages.

After ascending the platform, Father Theodor spoke briefly, explaining once more the meaning of this performance, this Mysteria. As we knelt, he prayed for the Holy Spirit's blessing.

The musicians tuned their instruments, then started playing a solemn overture.

Our Mysteria had begun.

A loud drumroll brought the overture to completion. Father Theodor opened the large tome of Latin Scriptures. We could hear the subtle rustle of parchment as he turned to the Gospels to read. His voice rolled over the silent crowd:

> Then they led Jesus from Caiaphas to the judgment hall; and it was early; but they themselves did not enter the judgment hall, lest they should be defiled and unable to eat the Passover.
>
> Pilate then went out to them, and said, What accusation do you bring against this man?

Judge Johann Holgert—as our own Pilate, the Roman procurator—loudly repeated the question: "What accusation do you bring against this man?" He spoke in German, as would all the participants in the Mysteria. He was at the center of the platform, garbed in a ceremonial mantle, wearing a crown of autumn-gold oak leaves and seated on his judge's bench, which had been moved out from our town hall for this purpose. His voice possessed the same assertive tone that was heard in his courtroom when he questioned litigating parties about their charges and pleas.

On each side of this Roman overlord stood his legionaries —to Judge Holgert's left, I with my spear; to the right, helmeted Klaus Zillendorf with his dagger. Both of us had clubs strapped to our belts. We kept our expressions impassive and businesslike.

Before us on the platform stood this Jesus—white-robed Lothar, his hands bound behind his back with leather straps.

The breeze from the mountains blew his wavy hair. Lowering his head, Lothar remained silent.

In response to the judge, Genscher the weaver—as high priest Caiaphas—shouted gruffly his Gospel lines: "If he were not a criminal, we would not have delivered him over to you!" He and Fleische the innkeeper—as high priest Annas—wore opulent liturgical vestments borrowed from Father Theodor.

I was startled at how much Genscher's sneer reminded me of the ugly bishop's grimace in the church's fresco.

Beside him, Fleische also spoke up: "It is not lawful for us to put any man to death!"

Father Theodor, reading from the Gospels, continued solemnly:

> Thus the saying of Jesus was fulfilled, which he
> spoke, signifying by what death he should die.

The two high priests moved away from the platform, having nothing more at present to say.

> Then Pilate entered into the judgment hall again,
> and summoned Jesus.

Judge Holgert stared at Lothar. "Are you the King of the Jews?"

I perked up my ears as this important dialogue began between Pontius Pilate and Jesus.

But Lothar remained silent, with head bowed. Had he forgotten his lines? But he knew these perfectly—I could swear to that! Memorizing was always easy for Lothar.

What's going on?

I stared at him. Something was happening to Lothar Lange. My impulsive guess was that Lothar's will, overwhelmed by his humility, was failing him. He couldn't force open his mouth to utter the divine words of our Savior.

But there's something more here also. Lothar at this moment

was starting to change. I only barely perceived this—yet it
was undeniable.

Lothar stayed silent—but the words of Jesus in response
to Pilate were nonetheless pronounced. Deacon Andreas Vogt,
seeing that something was wrong, found the only way out.
He took it upon himself to recite Jesus's lines to Pilate on
behalf of Lothar: "Do you ask this on your own, or did others
tell you about me?" The deacon's voice was strong.

Judge Holgert answered, "Am I a Jew? Your own nation
and the chief priests handed you over to me. What have
you done?"

"My kingdom is not of this world," Jesus answered,
through the voice of Andreas Vogt. Lothar stood motionless
before Pilate.

I could see that the spectators assumed everything was
proceeding as normal. Indeed, to me this might have been
even better. After all, Andreas Vogt was a deacon—more
qualified, I supposed, to speak the words of Jesus than unor-
dained Lothar.

The voice for Jesus continued: "If my kingdom were of
this world, my servants would fight to keep me from being
handed over to the Jews. But now my kingdom is not from
here."

Judge Holgert replied, "Are you then a king?"

Jesus answered, "As you say, I am a king. For this I was
born, and for this cause I came into the world, that I should
bear witness to the truth. Everyone who is of the truth hears
my voice."

Our Pilate shifted forward, his hands tightly gripping the
armrests of his bench. He appeared to be pondering some
difficult judgment in which neither party had provided
adequate evidence.

Finally, dramatically, he gave his dismissive answer:

"What is truth?"

All was silent.

I maintained my emotionless expression, but somehow I was shockingly struck by Pilate's question. In the stock-still crowd stretching out from the platform, I sensed the same impact. *What is truth?* hung in that day's gloomy air, a challenge to all.

That was the moment I first began to realize that it wasn't us staging the Mysteria, but rather the Mysteria was acting through us—exposing us, calling us to judgment. We of Rundschau were no longer actors and spectators; we had entered the realm of the original day of the cross, which dictated its own laws, its own causes and effects.

And before us stood a slender figure in a blindingly white robe with his head bowed.

What is truth? The question reverberating through the square demanded a decision: Who are you with? Are you among the crucifiers? Or will you be with the Crucified?

One or the other. There was no third choice.

Chapter 10
Behold the Man

AS IN SCRIPTURE, so also in our Mysteria: there was no spoken answer from the Savior to Pilate's question about truth.

After a dramatic pause, Deacon Vogt signaled the musicians. A booming drumroll came from the musicians' corner. Judge Holgert rose from his seat, wrapped his mantle about him, and went to the edge of the platform.

"I find in him no fault at all," he declared with finality. "But you have a custom at the Passover that I should release one man to you. Is it your will that I therefore release to you this King of the Jews?"

Our high priests cried out in answer: "Not this man, but Barabbas!"

> Now Barabbas was a robber.

> Pilate therefore took Jesus, and scourged him.

The procurator had given in. The devil had won this opening round.

The bagpipes droned, and flutes broke into a squeal.

Obeying an authoritative gesture from Judge Holgert, Klaus and I seized the convicted criminal by his arms and dragged him from the platform to the whipping post—where our Lord must suffer scourging.

We undid the leather straps binding Lothar's hands and tied him firmly against the post, then returned to our place next to Pilate's seat.

The drums rolled ominously.

And now I was shocked even more. I'd been privy to many details of the preparations, but I was in no way prepared for what happened next. Out of the crowd sprang a huge figure with a scarlet mask covering his entire head and neck. The darkly narrow eye-slits revealed nothing; it was impossible to tell who the actor was. And he brandished a whip. *A real whip!*

What in God's name is going on?

This masked figure faced the back of Lothar Lange, who stood with his hands overhead, tightly bound to the post. Lothar couldn't see his torturer. With horror I realized how delicate and defenseless his white back seemed before this monster appearing from nowhere.

After a moment's hesitation, the torturer took a swing. The whip, like a black snake, darted at Lothar's spine. The first blow rent the air with a deafening crack.

Lothar's body jerked convulsively at this blow.

The crowd gasped.

I, on the other hand, felt a sudden sense of relief. I could hardly refrain from laughing. How had I been so taken in? I should have figured it out right away.

Only two people in all Rundschau had perfected this trick —of cracking a whip an inch away from its target without causing the least harm. The first was the old shepherd Jürgen Zielmeister; the second was the blacksmith Karl Reinecke, who was taught this skill by Jürgen himself. The time had now come for good old Karl to demonstrate his mastery for the Lord's sake.

The shudder that ran down Lothar's spine at the first blow was not due to any pain, but only fear and surprise. After that, Lothar didn't move at all.

Karl Reinecke, however, hesitated longer with each blow. I easily imagined the apprehension he must have been feeling.

Ten blows were administered by Karl's steady hand. When he'd finished and turned to leave, I saw trembling in his powerful shoulders. He disappeared through the crowd.

Heinrich Fleische, the innkeeper's youngest son, approached the whipping post. He carried a small bucket and a brush. He dipped the brush, then made swaths of blood-red paint across Lothar Lange's white robe.

"Let us praise the suffering of our divine Savior for the redemption of our sins!" exclaimed Father Theodor, and the crowd knelt down to sing.

The sounds of a sacred hymn, like slow waves, rolled solemnly over Rundschau. But I was growing heavy-hearted; the moment was approaching for the beastliness that Klaus and I must show on our part. My heart sensed shame and repulsion. In my mind, I asked for forgiveness—from my friend, and from our merciful Lord.

Father Theodor read again from the Gospels.

> And the soldiers led Jesus away into the court called the Praetorium, and gathered their whole company around him. And they clothed him with purple, and made a crown of thorns, and put this on his head, saying, "Hail, King of the Jews!"
>
> And they beat his head with a reed, and spat upon him, and mocked him, bowing their knees to worship him.
>
> And having so mocked him, they took off from him the purple garment, and put his own clothes on him, and led him out to crucify him.

As music sounded, Klaus Zillendorf and I, with clubs in hand, descended from the platform and approached the post where Lothar was stretched out with his blood-stained back. We untied the straps on his hands.

Before the platform was a stool; lying across it was a red cloak. Klaus grabbed the cloak and threw it onto Lothar's shoulders. We shoved him onto the stool.

Nearby, on a special stand, lay the crown of real thorns. With care, Klaus and I together raised it from the stand; it pricked our fingers. While drums rolled in the background, we gently lowered it onto Lothar's head. I almost whispered: *Keep still, my brother, and it won't make you bleed.*

Into Lothar's right hand Klaus placed Judge Holgert's walnut staff—the symbol of governing authority in Rundschau. It represented the reed that the soldiers placed mockingly in the hands of Jesus.

The drums rolled again.

Klaus and I took the clubs from our belts, looked slowly in each other's faces, then turned reluctantly to Lothar. We hesitated.

Lothar gazed back at us. His face was pale; he bit his lower lip. Seeing our confusion, he came to our aid; he gave us a barely perceptible nod—as if to repeat what Jesus had said to the traitor Judas Iscariot: "What you are about to do, do quickly."

Do what must be done.

I raised my club over the shoulders of my best friend.

Almighty God, forgive us!

The drums rolled louder.

Distraught as we were, Klaus and I performed our role dutifully, swinging our clubs fiercely, yet barely making contact. Then we lowered our clubs and raised our hands to "slap" Lothar in the face, making sure we didn't disturb the dangerous crown of thorns. In conclusion we spat on the ground at his feet, then knelt before him and fairly screamed, "Hail, King of the Jews!"

My heart was pounding in my chest; I saw Klaus sweating and breathing heavily, as if he'd just finished chopping wood for the innkeeper's kitchen.

At last this portion of our nightmare was over. We snatched

the scarlet robe from Lothar's shoulders and yanked away the judge's walnut staff. If only we could have taken the crown too!

But Lothar wanted it this way; his cup, as the saying goes, was not yet full.

Klaus and I escorted our friend back to the platform. It was time for the drama's final event in the Praetorium.

Father Theodor turned the page in the Gospels.

> Then Pilate continued seeking to release him, but
> the Jews cried out...

Below us, the high priests Genscher and Fleische shouted lustily, "If you release this man you are no friend of Caesar's! Whosoever claims to be a king is speaking against Caesar!"

> Pilate therefore heard this, and he brought Jesus
> outside. He sat down in the judgment seat in a
> place that is called the Pavement, or in Hebrew,
> Gabbatha.

Judge Holgert rose again from his seat, his majestic figure towering over the scene. His voice thundered: "Behold, I bring him forth to you, that you may know I find no fault in him!" He stepped abruptly next to Lothar, took him by the elbow, and hustled him to the edge of the platform where all could see.

"Behold the *man!*" he roared.

At that moment, several designated people in the crowd were supposed to start shouting: "Crucify him!" A few voices began to mutter the words feebly, then immediately died out. The majority refused to utter a sound. The village of Rundschau was refusing to call for their Savior's crucifixion.

I heard Andreas Vogt whispering energetically to those nearby.

Fortunately, Genscher and Fleische found it in themselves to carry out their roles to the uttermost. "Crucify Him!"

their two voices cried out several times.

"Behold your king!" Judge Holgert yelled in response.

"Away with Him!" the high priests demanded. "Away with him! *Crucify!*"

"Shall I crucify your King?" The judge's voice betrayed genuine consternation.

The men snapped back, "We have no king but Caesar!"

Judge Holgert appeared to reel under the weight of unyielding fate. There was no avoiding it: this innocent One must die.

The high priests shouted again: "His blood be upon us and on our children!"

Judge Holgert summoned Klaus to bring a jug of water. Then he solemnly washed his hands over a basin. "Let everyone see!" he declared. "I am innocent of the blood of this man!"

The pipes played mournfully.

Judge Holgert left the platform. His shoulders stooped; he was majestic in posture no more, as if bent beneath some terrible burden.

As he passed near me, the judge for a moment raised his eyes. He was weeping.

Chapter 11
Everything Real

THE MOMENT HAD COME for the cross to make its entrance. Deacon Vogt waved his hand, the musicians played, and the crowd sang a hymn of the Holy Cross.

Lothar, crowned with thorns, descended from the platform. Klaus and I also stepped down and approached the cross, which was propped against the wall of Anton Stolz's house. We carried it solemnly back to the platform. In my hands the beechwood felt warm and alive.

Lothar stood waiting. His pale face looked drawn, but a peaceful light shone in his eyes. His gaze toward the cross seemed to say, "Here you are."

He got down on one knee and kissed the base of the cross. Then he turned, ready to take it upon his shoulder.

> And they laid on him his cross, and led him out to crucify him.

The procession of the cross, which passed down Rundschau's main street—from our Praetorium to our Golgotha— had been measured out by Deacon Vogt; it amounted, he informed us, to exactly five hundred paces. The evening before, he'd walked its length and laid down three marks with whitewash, one for each time our Lord Jesus would stumble and fall. At these points, Lothar was to stop and kneel, waiting for Father Theodor to read prayers and for the people to sing a hymn exalting the sacred suffering of our Savior. Afterward Klaus and I, his guards, were supposed to put our boots to Lothar's ribs, forcing him to get up and going.

But the Mysteria—as I increasingly grasped—would make its own corrections to our simple plans.

When Lothar took up the cross, he abruptly staggered under its weight—far beyond what could be expected. In the crowd, I found the pale face of Johann Vogel the carpenter. In his fearful eyes I detected a single question: "Oh, brother Lothar—could I possibly have blundered in my calculations?" All this staggering of Lothar's was strange indeed. Of course the cross was certainly not light, as Klaus and I could attest. But then Lothar was no weakling. How often I'd seen him haul grown rams upon his shoulders!

But now, clearly, the cross was close to crushing him.

He managed to stay on his feet, gasping pitifully, then took the first step. The people began singing *Via Sancta, Via Dolorosa, Te Gloriamus*: "Holy Way, Mournful Way, We Glorify You."

The procession of the cross had begun.

While the cross was heading to our village's main square, I wasn't quite myself. My head was ringing; my eyesight kept blurring. Yet I clearly recall how the procession was as beautiful and magnificent as it was sorrowful.

The onlookers had positioned themselves on both sides of the street. Father Theodor led the slow procession with the Gospels in his hands. He was followed by two boys in linen tunics who carried banners. Then came Lothar, bent beneath the cross, followed by Klaus and me as guards with our weapons in hand. Then came two more children carrying poles with ribboned garlands of fir boughs, followed by Anna-Maria Schubert, who portrayed the grieving mother of Jesus. On her head she wore a small crown that Bock the cooper had crafted from a tin hoop and polished brightly. Anna-Maria's gaze was tearful and downcast.

Throngs of Rundschau's residents brought up the rear.

Lothar's strained legs kept getting tangled in the hem of his white robe. I feared he'd never make it all the way.

Meanwhile my poor chaotic mind was imagining our street filled with a crowd of many thousands, whistling and howling, throwing stones and clods of earth.

We arrived at the white-marked spot for Christ's first fall. Lothar careened on wobbly legs, managed to straighten up, then lowered himself onto one knee and took a deep breath.

And here is where I apparently fell under a curse.

It came upon me as Father Theodor was reading words from the prophet Isaiah: "Like a lamb led to slaughter, like a sheep that before her shearers is silent, so he opened not his mouth." Klaus and I in that moment were supposed to kick and thrash Lothar severely, then force him to his feet to get on with carrying his cross. I positioned my foot to administer the first "kick."

Then a heated, murky, malicious wave engulfed my soul. I felt I'd lost control of myself, as if an evil spirit was assaulting my mind, my muscles, my hands, my feet. Its voice roared in my head: *What are you waiting for? Trounce him! Finish him! Crack his ribs; crush his spine beneath your heel.*

"Make it realistic," Deacon Andreas had coached us this week. "Everything real!"

Before me was my best friend—yet I was quite ready to batter and break him. This flash of desire seemed as genuine as any I'd ever known.

Everything real! This is your role! Don't be a weakling, get to it!

This attack upon me was so unexpected, the voice so brazen and impudent, its demands so unnatural and perverse— that after a moment of confusion my soul exploded with fury. From deep within, a greater voice bellowed: "Whoever you are—*be gone!*"

The spell faded, as if it had never been.

I came to my senses, where I stood with my foot still poised to strike. My kick never came to pass.

I don't give a tinker's damn whether this is realistic. I reached down to Lothar, to lend a hand with his cross, and to help him get up.

From the moments immediately following, I recall only fragments. I remember music, and gusting breezes, and intent faces on both sides of our way to the cross.

Lothar soon reached the spot appointed for his second fall. He was about to drop to one knee when suddenly he lost his balance and nearly fell over sideways with the cross. He barely caught himself dropping onto both knees and thrusting his right hand to the ground for support.

At that moment, the cross's shifting weight pressed against Lothar's thorn-crowned head. I saw blood on his brow. Klaus and I froze, not knowing what to do. Yet the Mysteria had to go on.

Then it was as if an angel had rushed to the side of the cross. This angel was my Veronika, who dashed from the crowd holding a white cloth, though her appearance was supposed to occur later.

Veronika cried as she wiped Lothar's face with the cloth. She was so beautiful at that moment—as if she held her heart in her hands. So it seemed to me.

Again I helped Lothar to his feet. The procession continued, though it was apparent Lothar was finding this more and more difficult. Blood kept trickling from where the thorns stung his head. I stayed at his side and helped as I could.

Finally we came to the spot for his third fall. Here Lothar collapsed, with the cross pinning down his body. The crowd gasped.

Klaus and I quickly eased the cross off of him. Lothar managed to get up. Father Theodor and Deacon Vogt hurried to his side, but he shook his head as if to say he must and could continue on. But another hundred paces remained till we would reach the Golgotha platform.

Father Theodor stood beside the paused procession. As planned, he again opened the Gospels to read.

> And as they led him onward, they seized one
> Simon of Cyrene coming in from the country. And
> they forced him to carry the cross behind Jesus.

This, for me, was another cue. I was to arrest this Simon of Cyrene from the crowd and put him to work. However, in the strangeness of how everything was playing out, my blurred mind completely forgot who was playing Simon.

Nevertheless I hoisted my spear and stepped into the crowd. Impulsively I seized a man by the collar and dragged him out to where Klaus waited; the top of the cross's vertical beam was resting in my fellow soldier's clasped hands.

I scarcely believed it when I finally observed the face of the man I'd abducted. It was the carpenter Joachim Vogel, maker of this cross.

Chapter 12
Hour of Reckoning

YES, I HAD LEARNED THIS: nothing in our Mysteria was happening by chance.

As bagpipes droned, Joachim Vogel placed his shoulder under the instrument of torture he'd fashioned with his own hands.

Our procession slowly moved onto the main square—to our Golgotha, to the place where I must commit today's most heinous deed. Here I would crucify my closest friend.

Christ, have mercy on me!

The crowd flowed into the square and encircled the platform under a sky now entirely overcast. The damp wind cut through my chain mail, chilling me. I looked at Klaus, catching in his eyes the same lonely anxiety that gripped me.

We had arrived. The hour of reckoning had come. What had occurred so many centuries ago in the Holy Land would here be reenacted—with an important difference. Now we would do it with our own hands.

Have mercy, Lord; have mercy upon us!

From his appointed reading place, Father Theodor's voice boomed across the square:

> And when they came to the place which is called Golgotha, there they crucified him.
>
> And an inscription was placed over him: "This is the King of the Jews."

Silence filled the square where the procession halted.

Joachim Vogel hauled the cross onto the platform, carefully laid it upon the wooden surface, then jumped down.

It was our turn. Klaus and I climbed up, leading Lothar.

At that moment my confused mind finally cleared. From up here, on the platform crowning the highest point in Rundschau, I could look out—and the entire district seemed visible. Not far from the village, the gentle slope of the valley opened, reaching toward foothills bedecked with a colorful autumn shroud of fir trees, larches, and hornbeams. In the distance were tiny white dots—the flock of Rundschau sheep under the watch of old man Jürgen.

The horizon beyond seemed boundless—I imagined it stretching hundreds and thousands of leagues. I imagined innumerable human lives, all their smoldering passions, all their suffering and prayers.

All this world now centered upon Rundschau's main square—upon Golgotha.

Lothar bent his knees, kissed the cross, and spread himself upon it. I had no strength to link my eyes to his.

My heart felt squeezed as if in a vise. Imagining the rusty nails, I began with hesitant hands to bind Lothar's wrists with leather straps. My fingers, it seemed, refused to obey. I regained control, reminding myself that if I didn't do everything correctly, it could easily cause Lothar additional suffering.

"Forgive me," my lips whispered. "Forgive me."

At last it was finished. The straps fit into special grooves Joachim had notched for this purpose. We drew the straps tighter.

Then I nailed the sign above Lothar's head. He winced as each hammer blow jolted through the timber beneath his head and back.

From the crowd, mighty Karl Reinecke the blacksmith came up, this time wearing no mask. He assisted Klaus and me in raising our cross with this man upon it. We gently lowered its base into the socket Joachim Vogel had prepared.

Lothar's pale profile, with outstretched arms, was there above us, hovering over the square like a white bird.

The bagpipes sounded.

All across the square, people knelt.

Klaus and I stood motionless on our silent watch, flanking the cross. I glanced upward. On Lothar's temple and brow, dribbles of blood from his thorn wounds ran down, flowing onto his sunken cheek.

A moment earlier, I couldn't bear to look upon his face; now I couldn't turn away.

Lothar bit his lower lip. He gazed out over our rooftops; his eyes seemed violet instead of blue. I felt that he wasn't just gazing into the gloomy distance; he saw something.

Father Theodor read again from the Gospels:

> And the soldiers cast lots to divide his garments.

> And the people stood by, watching; but the rulers scoffed at him, saying…

"He saved others," declared Genscher the weaver; "let him save himself, if he is the Christ of God, his Chosen One!"

The wind blew its mournful song. I heard weeping in the crowd.

I saw Joachim Vogel quite close to us, as if he had to remain near this cross, his workmanship, now that the hour of its dreadful purpose had come.

To the platform came Anna-Maria Schubert as Mary the Mother of God. She stood motionless before the cross. Anna-Maria's face was as pale as Lothar's, and she seemed immersed in prayer.

The people sang *Stabat Mater Dolorosa*—"The Sorrowful Mother Stood…"

Next to Anna-Maria stood young Peter Hofbauer as John, the Lord's beloved disciple.

Margreta Bern—Mary Magdalene—also came near. She sat at the foot of the cross, embracing its glowing wood. Her eyes also glowed with peace, as if she were the real Mary Magdalene after the Lord had cast out of her those seven demons.

Father Theodor read more.

> And at the cross of Jesus, there stood his mother, and Mary Magdalene.
>
> When Jesus therefore saw his mother, and the disciple whom he loved also standing nearby, he spoke unto his mother…

"Woman, behold your son!"

> Then he said to the disciple…

"Behold your mother!"

Again these words of Jesus were uttered on his behalf— and Lothar's—by Deacon Andreas. My friend's silence seemed more profound than ever, as if Lothar himself had stepped aside.

I watched him. Yes, he seemed absent—no longer with us. It occurred to me that his humble soul perhaps had yielded its place, giving it back to the One who alone had the right to occupy this cross of crucifixion. And who, perhaps, was even now descending from heaven above to make his appearance among us.

Father Theodor's voice sounded:

> After this, Jesus—knowing that all things were now accomplished, and so that Scripture might be fulfilled—said…

Our deacon's voice gave the cry: "I thirst."

> Now a vessel of vinegar was sitting there; one of the men took a sponge, filled it with vinegar, and

> put it upon a stalk of hyssop, and lifted it to the
> mouth of Jesus.

I snapped out of my stupor as if someone had struck me. Klaus handed me the wet sponge. Hardly aware anymore of what I was doing, I stuck it on the end of my spear and raised it to Lothar's chin. He didn't move.

Deathly silence hovered over the square.

Suddenly his body twitched, then tautened like a string. Klaus and I again were stupefied, unable to move.

Lothar lifted his face to the sky. His eyes blazed with blue flame, as if they reflected eternal light from beyond all clouds, beyond the heavens themselves. At this same moment a narrow breach appeared in the gray overcast above us, a pale rift slowly opening in swirls of mist.

My friend's face seemed transformed into a holy countenance—I don't know how else to put it. It showed sorrow and pain, but also warmth and love and meekness—and *humanity*. I was sure I was seeing a man's face in divine ecstasy.

Vaguely I heard once more Father Theodor's voice, narrating again from Scripture these awful events, guiding them toward a finale, their inexpressible and frightening resolution.

> And Jesus said…

Suddenly a great, strong voice rang out over the main square of Rundschau. It was at once the voice of my friend—young and clear—yet also a new, previously unheard voice: mighty, pure, like the sound of a silver trumpet.

"*Father!* Father, forgive them! For they know not what they do!"

Deacon Vogt, who'd been about to recite this line for Lothar, seemed frozen with his mouth wide open.

We were hearing the voice of the Lord from the cross. It penetrated the depths of our souls, stirring us like a river's strong fresh current.

That voice deepened:

"*Eli, Eli, lama sabachthani!* My God! My God! Why have you forsaken me?"

It seemed to me then that even the distant white Alpine peaks shuddered at the inner power of this cry from the cross.

The crowd on the square was hushed and still. The wind had died in the air, and then another cry from the cross reverberated over us:

"It is finished! It is finished! *It is finished!*"

Through the brightening gap in the clouds over our heads, a golden ray of sun shone down, illuminating the square and the people. It was like a gentle hand caressing the head of a child.

Seconds later, as the sunbeam began fading, there came one last cry:

"Father! *Father!* Into your hands I commit my spirit!"

The sunlight vanished; the clouds closed the breach in their gray ranks.

Silence hung over the square. I was on my knees before the cross. All around the square, people at that moment were kneeling, and many wept.

The body on the cross twitched again, then drooped. The pale face beneath the crown of thorns fell forward.

I saw a drop of blood tear itself away from Lothar's chin and splash onto the wooden platform.

I lifted my eyes, looking closer. I saw Lothar's legs go limp, no longer supporting his weight.

My friend had fainted!

Close by, I heard the whisper of Vogel the carpenter cursing himself. Yet this was certainly not his fault; how could he ever have imagined Lothar might lose consciousness? I saw Vogel's face become deathly pale—as if he also might faint.

Lothar's body hung in a most unnatural position, although his face—eyes closed—seemed peacefully composed.

What must we do?

The Mysteria once again proved to us that the Lord himself was directing these actions.

A harsh croaking sound rang out over our heads—the laughter of Konrad Eisenstein.

I turned as if a hornet had stung my neck. Konrad stood near the front of the crowd. While laughing, he stared intently at the man on the cross.

He clapped several times, then loudly exclaimed: "Bravo! Magnificently performed! *Bravo!*" He chuckled again, turned, and went away.

Konrad Eisenstein had said little, but the effect was shattering. It was as if some ethereal force uniting us all had suddenly receded. Konrad had broken the spell.

The musicians saved the day. Bagpipes began playing *Te Deum Laudamus*—"You, O Lord, We Praise"—and as this hymn was taken up by the people's voices, our Mysteria returned. Slowly, once again, the village of Rundschau faded from view; we were again at Golgotha in the Holy Land, on the day and hour of our divine redemption.

Father Theodor, unaffected by Konrad's interruption, read once more from the Gospels in his voice of warm authority.

> Then one of the soldiers pierced the side of Jesus with a spear, and at once blood and water came forth.
>
> One who saw this has borne witness; his testimony is true, and he knows he speaks truthfully—that you also might believe.

According to plan, these were to be the last spoken words of our Mysteria. However, one more act remained.

I rose from my knees. I stared at Lothar; even with his frame so awkwardly stretched and strained, I saw the faint rise and fall of his breathing chest.

The wooden tip of my Roman spear touched Lothar's ribs.

Immediately, on Deacon Vogt's signal, a choir of children's voices began singing a hymn composed by Judge Holgert specifically for our Mysteria:

> Lamb of God, Holy Jesus—
> He accepted death in his love for us,
> He defied death on the glorious cross,
> And gave salvation to the world.
> Glory, glory, meek Lamb of the Father!
> Glory, glory, Savior ours!
> Hallelujah!

While these clear and simple words washed over the crowd's souls like a summer rain after a long drought, those of us closest to the cross became more urgently heedful of the fact that Lothar Lange was indeed unconscious; it was growing ever more dangerous for him to continue hanging there.

So it was that our Mysteria gained two additional scenes that weren't there in the original scenario: the descent from the cross, and the resurrection.

With careful haste, Klaus and I—helped by Joachim Vogel and Paul Hofbauer—undid the straps holding Lothar up. We saw how the leather straps had cut deeply enough into his wrists to draw blood.

We lowered the limp body into the arms of Reinecke the blacksmith and Genscher the weaver. They in turn laid out Lothar on the platform, where someone had placed a soft woolen cloak.

A swelling group of villagers came closer, watching anxiously.

I held up Lothar's head while Deacon Andreas tenderly, almost maternally, removed the crown of thorns from Lothar's injured brow. Handing the crown to Father Theodor, the deacon slapped Lothar's cheeks and splashed water in his face from a jar someone had brought us.

We watched in nervous silence.

Then Lothar opened his eyes. Murmurs of relief sounded all around.

He looked at us. For an instant, I saw acute fear in his eyes. But the jubilant looks on our faces seemed to put his mind at ease.

The musicians struck up a lively tune. Soon everyone around us was congratulating each other for the Mysteria's success. Lothar, of course, who by now was sitting up dazedly, got the lion's share of attention.

Not that he really noticed.

As the crowd eased back and gave him more room, I stayed at Lothar's side. He seemed to be in a state of extreme confusion. He could remember nothing at all of what had happened to him on the cross—nothing!

From his bewildered words, I learned the source of the fear I'd seen in his eyes when he first came to consciousness: "I thought something went wrong and stopped the Mysteria, and it was all my fault. I was sure I'd ruined everything." I could see that Lothar still imagined this might indeed be the case, despite my assurances otherwise.

I helped him to his feet. Then Father Theodor stepped near; he'd been moving through the crowd, embracing the Mysteria's participants. He did so with Lothar, and kissed his forehead.

People nearby spoke to me, drawing my attention away from Lothar. They voiced their impressions of this day, describing their feelings during various scenes. "All so astounding," they said; "so much like a miracle."

When I looked again for Lothar, I discovered only the red-streaked robe lying neatly folded on the edge of the platform. Resting upon it was the crown; dried blood showed on several thorns.

Lothar I couldn't find.

Chapter 13
No Other Path

WITH THIS CONCLUSION to the wonder that had been our Mysteria, everyone moved into the church, where a benedictory mass was held to offer thanksgiving for what had transpired; for as Father Theodor put it, "A true act of grace fell upon us." Afterward a modest dinner was held at Eberhard Fleische's inn for our guests from other villages, whom we then walked to the edge of Rundschau as they headed home. Then gray clouds burst forth with showers; hurriedly we took down street decorations before they were ruined by rain.

Finally, as evening approached, I shed my legionary's outfit and set out to look for Lothar.

I knew where to look.

Lothar was at the abandoned farm half a league from Rundschau, in the barn he'd refurbished for the Waldheim sheep. He was sitting in the farthest corner, caressing the neck of one of those sheep.

The barn inside was warm and quiet; the sheep had eaten their fill of hay and were dozing. I carefully stepped my way among them to sit down next to Lothar.

"Everyone's looking for you," I said.

"You didn't tell them where I was?"

As if I would! I shook my head.

For a while we didn't speak. Then Lothar asked softly, "Did father bring in the flock?"

"I saw him returning—just as I left the village."

Again we fell into silence. I heard snorts from some of the sheep. One was chewing hay. Lothar was lost in his thoughts, and I didn't want to interrupt. Finally he spoke again.

"This has been excruciating."

I faced him and nodded, welcoming whatever he might care to explain to me.

He craned his neck to gaze into the rafters. "How can I express it? Bearing that cross…"

He hesitated. I waited.

"I always knew my soul was as nothing before the face of the Lord. But under that cross, it was *shown* to me—just how unworthy I happen to be."

He stroked the sheep before him, then sighed again.

"Arnie, it's *hard*—having that shown to me. It's like the judgment, like when a person dies and all his life gets exposed—it feels like that."

After yet another silence, Lothar shook his head and whispered in an altered voice: "Oh, but what *love* it is!"

He seemed unable to speak another word.

After darkness deepened, I rose, pressed a hand to his shoulder, then left, trying not to trip over the sleeping flock.

Hours later, asleep in our attic at home, I fell into a nightmare.

I was once again in soldier's garb—not chain mail this time, or a leather cap with a feather, but rather laminated armor and a heavy helmet. In the Praetorium's courtyard, under torrid light, I was surrounded by other soldiers.

Before me—was the Lord.

He was seated, wearing a scarlet robe and crown of thorns, his head bowed. I mocked him while my rough-faced comrades laughed. I spat in his downcast face. I landed blows on fresh wounds from his earlier scourging. I grabbed a staff and beat him about the head, driving those thorns deeper into his flesh. Blood streamed onto his robe.

But unlike the similar scene in our Mysteria, this time I

felt not the least hint of trepidation. Oh, no! Shouts from the others egged me on; it was if I'd gone mad. I had no desire to restrain myself as I delivered blow after blow, each more vicious than the last. My wicked joy was tinged by hopelessness—but this only bolstered my fury.

Little by little, some portion of my soul began recognizing each strike as a sin—no different from millions of sins I'd committed since the day of my birth.

Another blast of my fist to his temple—*another sin.*

Another plug of my spit to his cheeks—*another sin.*

It seemed this could go on forever, but my resourcefulness was finally spent. My mocking ceased.

Then the Lord lifted his gaze to me.

I jerked awake, in the middle of the night, in tears and a cold sweat.

At dawn, the sun's first rays hadn't yet fallen on the town hall square when I was knocking on Father Theodor's door. He'd hardly opened the door when I threw myself at his feet, demanding that he impose the most severe penance upon me. There was no sinner on earth, I told him, more wicked and miserable than I, the cursed Arnold Enke. I poured out for him a catalog of countless sins I recalled from my twenty years.

Father Theodor heard me out, then remained silent awhile. Finally he recited a prayer for forgiveness and told me to go home.

I hesitated.

He took me by the shoulders. "Go home, my child, and sin no more." He required no penance, but asked me to make every effort to pray more often.

From there I walked to the church, which was empty. There was only silence under the old arches.

I stood before the fresco portraying the procession of the

cross. I looked again at the image of the Lord. I was fascinated —as I'd been so often before—by how serene the countenance of our Savior could be while carrying his cross to Golgotha, surrounded by that hellish crowd. In his face was neither pain nor wrath. No disappointment, no despair. Only peace and beaming light. Why?

Gradually I let go any thoughts of this mystery. My soul became as empty and quiet as the church. I listened to the silence.

That's when the Voice rang out.

It did so without disturbing the silence. To be precise, I heard nothing with my bodily ears. The Voice sounded somewhere deep inside me, peaceful and majestic. It seemed to both heal my heart and burn it at the same time, just as icy waters of the Kreuzbach brook simultaneously refresh and sting one's skin.

The Voice spoke as if in response to all my unvoiced questions.

"If you would be perfect, deny yourself, take up your cross, and follow me."

But what does this mean—"perfect"?

"Possessing eternal life. Throwing off the shackles of death and decay, and conquering time. Knowing the meaning of creation and your entry into it. Conquering hell and the devil. Finding the love of my Father and dwelling there forever. Sitting at my right hand to reign with me.

"I've laid out the way for you, my child. You need only follow. All is given through the cross."

The cross?

"Yes."

Being crucified?

"Yes."

Is there no other way?

"Coming to earth—coming to *you*—I myself chose no other path. No other path is higher. In a world that does not know God, only the cross reveals the way. There is no other."

The fresco came into my awareness once more, with the calm countenance of Christ there—so mystifying.

"My triumph," the Voice explained. "My victory. It was my desire to carry the cross and to be crucified, for my love cannot be contained. I am the crucified God, and my love is of the cross."

The voice sounded luminous and serene, like a warm wind wafting through the first leaves of April.

"Henceforth you and I are one. I live within you—I am crucified within you. Such is my love for you, my son."

Were these words really spoken, or did I imagine them? I don't know. But they were imprinted upon my soul, and I determined that throughout whatever years were granted me on this earth by the grace of God, I would ponder them—so that somehow I might begin to understand.

Chapter 14
Seal of Suffering

I WAS HELPING the men of Rundschau in disassembling the Mysteria's platforms. These had remained standing for a few days as a nostalgic reminder for us all, but now everything was coming down.

As I carefully laid an armful of dislodged planks in a pile, I heard Father Theodor's voice behind me.

"Arnold, my child, I suppose you'll be seeing Lothar Lange today, right? Ask him to come see me. I wish to speak with him."

I soon found Lothar. Because of the woodcarving skills he'd been taught by old Jürgen, he'd been assisting Joachim Vogel with piecework in his carpentry shop, and was just now leaving.

"Father Theodor wants to talk with you. Again."

Lothar nodded. As we turned together toward the square, he grinned. "And you wonder—just what could he and I be discussing that we meet about it so often these days? Eh?"

"You're right, Lothar. I'm curious. It must be important."

"It must be. But I haven't understood it much, Arnie. He talks about anointing, and the mystery of the cross. He says I can expect some unexpected turns—that's exactly how he put it, *unexpected turns.* He said I shouldn't be confused or afraid of what comes."

Lothar said no more. As we walked side by side, I realized my friend's life could no longer follow its former path. It was taking on some new dimension that I was not a part of.

Unwilling to settle for silence between us, I brought up a different subject. "They say Bertha Zellermann is completely recovered. The council has found her a house; they'll help her get back on her feet."

"Then it's time," Lothar responded. As if to compensate for his reticence on our earlier topic, he now explained to me in detail his plan for returning Frau Bertha's sheep to her. It was to be carried out in secret.

"But the woman ought to know how you've helped her," I responded. "Why keep it hidden?"

"Because it's the right thing to do."

"No! Tell the truth—that's what right."

"Not this time," he insisted.

"Don't be so foolish! People should hear what's happened."

"No."

"Yes! Let Rundschau and the whole district finally realize what kind of person Lothar Lange is!"

He groaned, rolling his eyes.

"Don't be over-humble," I scolded. "On this matter, you've earned whatever praise you get. Let them *know!*"

The blueness blazed in Lothar's eyes. "I will *not*, Arnie. That's final."

I gave this further thought. "Alright, you will not. But I'll go this very day and speak the truth to Frau Bertha, who deserves to hear it."

That was it. My friend was enraged. We were near a straw-pile beside Fleische's inn, and Lothar shoved me into it, wrestling me down.

His unexpected ferocity somewhat dampened my resolve.

Holding me down, Lothar calmed himself. "Please, Arnie, understand! If everyone finds out, they'll start treating me like some Saint Nicholas. They'll keep expecting more from me. And more! And more!"

He let me go once I swore myself to secrecy.

A few mornings later, at the house of Granny Krause

where Bertha was staying until her new house was ready, the two women rushed into the yard to see what all the commotion was about. A large flock of healthy sheep was there, with the Waldheim mark colored on their wool. Frau Bertha fainted right then and there.

Whenever this story was told within my hearing (which was often—and everyone in some way associated this miracle with the Mysteria), I never once made the slightest remark upon it.

This good deed toward Bertha Zellermann—miraculous or otherwise—seemed to be a hallmark of what Rundschau was becoming. In the first weeks after the Mysteria, our village was like a model of virtue—not the kind typically associated with monasteries and churches, but something simple, sincere, and humble. For in Rundschau—so graciously delivered from the plague raging around us, even after inviting people from infected villages to come witness our Mysteria—we'd become more like a family than ever.

Previously, if the widow Martha Bierhof had asked Peter Mischhold for neighborly help in fixing the roof of her barn, Peter would have frowned, given a sideways glance into the sky, and directed their conversation toward the proper compensation for such an onerous task. He and the widow would have spent the morning dickering before Peter finally donned his cap and went to inspect the barn. But now when she made this request (which I overheard in the square), Peter smiled and replied, "Of course, Martha, with the greatest pleasure."

In Eberhard Fleische's inn, where we'd always heard conversation about hunting, the harvest, the ailments of our livestock and our various relatives, and the virtues and shortcomings in figure and character of some of our village's girls, the Mysteria became the favorite topic of discussion. Each scene was relived, and men told exactly where they'd stood and what they'd felt. From behind the bar where Eberhard listened, he nodded in a dignified way—after all, it was he who had donated the famous timbers from which the Mysteria's cross was made.

Even Konrad Eisenstein seemed transformed in those days. He started attending mass, where he would stand throughout the service and listen attentively. Some of our village matrons found this highly moving. They made a fuss over Konrad, welcoming him to their homes to feed him. Father Theodor, however, seemed to have little confidence in the sincerity of Konrad's supposed conversion.

Konrad seemed peculiarly drawn to Lothar, often finding ways to encounter him in the streets, where he greeted him with excessive friendliness. As Lothar moved on, Konrad gazed after him a long while.

"He follows me like a shadow," Lothar complained to me. "Even in church, I get no peace. His eyes drill holes right through me."

"Give him a thrashing," I advised. "At least verbally. Then he'll back off."

"I get the feeling he wouldn't. No, Arnie, there's more going on here. I just don't know what." Lothar continued showing Konrad respect.

It was in these days that our village matrons began prattling more excessively than ever about Lothar's noble and godly attributes. This evolved over time into greater efforts to take him under their wing. Lothar's attempt to keep his distance only aroused them further.

As Lothar became aware of their words and designs, I saw how they darkened his mood, causing him to withdraw even further within himself. And if anyone started talking about the Mysteria in his presence, he either sat there silently, staring into space, or slipped away unnoticed.

I myself would sometimes come upon Lothar and discover a look in his eyes that frightened me; this look bore a hidden seal of suffering I couldn't break. Some sort of pain had settled into him. I hoped desperately he was finding relief where he most often sought it—in church and in discussions with Father Theodor.

Lothar was often seen at dawn emerging from the church —which meant (so people reasoned) that he'd spent all night there. This seemed especially odd to the matrons, who universally agreed it was high time Lothar got married.

In a strange way, he was maturing before all our eyes. He'd grown into a man, and I mean not just outwardly, but inwardly. Sometimes his face glowed with an amazing serenity; his eyes would possess a paternal kindness. His exalted gaze could give anyone a lift. He was not yet twenty-one years old, and still a shepherd—but at times in his demeanor he appeared to be thirty-five and nothing less than a knight.

Chapter 15
Village Idiot

ELSEWHERE, THE PLAGUE was finally passing. So it was that several of my comrades and I found ourselves in Linden toward the end of November. The magistrate there had summoned healthy male volunteers from surrounding districts to help establish order. Seven or eight of us from Rundschau answered the call.

I went, while Lothar stayed in Rundschau with old Jürgen.

Linden had become truly an awful sight, and we more deeply realized how fortunate we had been in Rundschau, by God's great mercy. The city had lost a quarter of its population to the plague. The gaping doors and windows of empty houses, the garbage-strewn streets, the bonfires on the squares, the smell of decay hanging in the air despite cold winds from the Alps—all this filled me with despondency. There were no longer corpses in the streets—the town's burial brigades had done their job. But the town looked like a war zone. The people's faces and posture conveyed despair and lingering terror.

We Rundschau men were assigned various tasks: raking out heaps of ashes and debris after the fires, removing furniture from abandoned and ransacked houses, and cleaning the barracks that had served as a public hospital during the plague.

While we worked, we sensed the echo of death everywhere. The town's surviving leaders had plunged themselves into the reestablishment of order, but the entire effort seemed to be just another funeral. We were burying the town's past, entombing the life that existed before the plague. It would be preserved now only in memory as the "good old days"; better ones might never come to pass.

When the first snows came, we returned to Rundschau. Our journey back was marked by encounters with menacing packs of stray dogs. They seemed to have flooded into our district, coming from God knows where.

My home village now seemed to me a refuge of peace and goodness, though the horror I'd experienced in Linden stayed imprinted in my heart.

But, in fact, Rundschau was changing too. For one thing, it was expanding. On the edges of Rundschau, the sound of axes at work could be heard, as new settlers built houses. Reports had spread that our village was a blessed place miraculously spared from the epidemic, so people left their less fortunate locations to seek a new and better life among us. We accepted and helped them as best we could.

I was quite glad to see Lothar after my long absence in Linden. With winter settling in, he no longer took the sheep out to pasture; he spent most of his daylight hours as a contract laborer, sometimes disappearing for further conversations with Father Theodor.

At Lothar's home on my second evening back in Rundschau, I was greeted by old man Zielmeister with a pat on the shoulder and a joke or two. A fire crackled in the hearth. Lothar had set the supper table, and was sitting with his back against the wall, eyeing me. The hearth cast an orange glow upon his face; in that moment, for the first time, he truly looked like a stranger to me, with a stamp of otherworldliness more pronounced than ever. Or did I only imagine it? One sees all sorts of things in a room illumined only by a fireplace.

We talked about this and that. Old Jürgen, after having a bite to eat with us, went off to bed. Then with Lothar, I went into greater detail about the horrors I'd seen in Linden. Lothar sank into silence and a distant stare, nodding along to my story.

When I finished, he said, "Maybe I should have gone with you."

"Your place was here," I answered. "And still is."

"I don't know anymore where I should be," he replied. "Something's out of kilter." His voice carried a strange tone. "You've no doubt heard that many here think I'm crazy."

I was unsure how to respond.

Lothar smiled. "The village idiot, that's me. Touched in the head." He stuck out his tongue, crossed his eyes, and shook his head.

I was flabbergasted. "Brother, be serious!"

Stern-faced, he got up to pace the room.

I mumbled, "Someone in Rundschau actually thinks you're *insane?*"

"What else?"

"I can't believe it."

"Neither could I at first." He kept pacing. "But then, judge for yourself.

"First of all, I'm almost twenty-one but still not engaged, still not promised to anyone. And despite the boundless efforts of Margreta Bern and her friends, I haven't the slightest interest in any of their daughters.

"Second, I'm praying too much—in the church at midnight, or getting with Father Theodor during the day."

Lothar seated himself on the bench across the table from me. His voice was quieter. "Number three: I *have* acted strangely for a while, as you well know. And of course folks have to figure out why. They say it's the Mysteria, since they well remember what I did that day. So they started saying I've let it go to my head—gotten full of myself. But somehow this doesn't seem exactly it. So now they've come to the exact opposite conclusion: my head's empty."

I was astounded. "What on earth!" I exclaimed. "Who cares what silly old women think of you? How about others? Judge Holgert? Karl Reinecke? Joachim Vogel? Deacon Andreas? And my own father, and Father Theodor! What about them?"

"They treat me well," Lothar said. "But then again, most people do. I'm actually treated better than ever. Though likely it's because everyone's thinking, *It's a sin to kick someone when he's down.*"

In bewilderment, I stared at Lothar. "But you know you're fine. And I know. And the judge and my father and Father Theodor and the other men—we all know it."

"Well, that's just the thing," Lothar said gloomily. "I'm *not* fine."

Again I stared, waiting for his explanation.

Lothar gazed into the fire. "So much has changed inside me. I see differently." He placed his elbows on the table and propped his chin on his fists. "In the Mysteria, I dropped into —I don't even know how to describe it. Into some deep abyss. Hell?

"I would never have said such a thing before, but now I feel I know what hell is. What it's *like* there."

Lothar spoke with such quiet, persuasive power, I didn't doubt his truthfulness for even an instant.

"It was all inside me that day, opened up to me. My soul was revealed to me, right to the core—and there in my soul was the underworld. I'm amazed I survived."

His voice lowered. "Carrying the cross, I was walking that abyss totally alone. Nothing else there—no streets of Rundschau, no crowd, no you, no Father Theodor. No earth. No heaven. Even God wasn't there.

"It has to be worse than death, Arnie, believe me. And then my sins started showing themselves. To *me*. I saw *my* guilt—my share in crucifying our Lord. My God! And I re-membered how much I once *wanted* all those sins.

"I realized in that hour what kind of judgment I'd brought down on myself. So terrible, I wanted to howl." Lothar looked at me gravely. "If you informed me now that in the Mysteria I started howling under the cross like a wolf, I wouldn't be surprised."

The fireplace again drew his gaze. "In that abyss, I had only one thought: I'm perishing in this darkness, and I *deserve* it. And I *hate* him, and I hate myself, and I hate everything else that torments me. But there's nowhere else to go, and nothing I can do."

The frown receded from Lothar's face. "And then he re-vealed himself to me."

"He?"

"The Lord." He leaned back. "I can't explain. It was as if, for one instant, he *looked* at me. One glance. And in one glance —there was *everything*." Lothar pronounced this last word in a rapturous whisper.

"I never imagined anyone could see me like that, under-stand me like that. *Me*, even *me*, a poor sinner as you well know. I'm still in a daze. It's that kind of love.

"Then I understood: that's how he looks at all of us: at you, at me, at Konrad, at our wretched old gossips. *Boundless mercy.*

"But there's another thing I've realized. To see it—this love—you have to go through this hell as well. And God is infinitely sorry for us, but there's no other way."

Lothar positioned himself more comfortably on the bench, with his legs tucked beneath him.

"And now, looking at others—it seems to me I understand them in their deepest being. I sense affliction in their souls, their torment, whatever causes them to suffer. *And I can't tell them about it.* They all, you see, have some kind of sorrow in their heart. And the cause of that sorrow is sin, and people can't escape from it until they acknowledge it, and want to escape. So *He* suffers along with them, being closer to us than we are to ourselves—feeling everything!

"I catch this, Arnie—and my heart starts to bleed. And it drives me crazy.

"If only they could experience his glance! One look from him is enough—he is God after all—and then all our suffering becomes like a shadow, like a dream. And all that remains is —his *love*."

He pressed his palms onto the tabletop. There was agony in his voice. "I can't explain it; it's so impossible! That's why he went onto the cross—there was no other way for him to express it. But who knows this? I myself can't see how to deal with it. It rips me up inside. Arnie, if only you knew!"

"I—I *know*," I said softly.

Lothar eyed me strangely, then looked again into the dwindling fire. "I love you all as I never have before. But what exactly I should do now—I can't decide."

"What does Father Theodor say?"

Lothar nodded. "That I should endure and be patient, and the Lord himself will take care of everything. So here I wait— while half the village thinks I've lost my mind."

It was well after midnight when our conversation ended, and Lothar walked me to the gate. In the clear cold sky, a slender moon shone above distant slopes white with snow. From along the road to Linden came the howling of stray dogs.

Lothar gave a friendly parting punch to my shoulder. "Brother," he said, "don't worry about me." That was a request I couldn't guarantee.

Then behind me I heard snow crunching; in the same instant, Lothar's face darkened as he looked over my shoulder. I turned.

Konrad Eisenstein stood twenty paces away from us. From his throat came something like a repressed laugh or cough.

"Good evening, Lothar my boy!" he said. His voice made me think he might be drunk; perhaps the reformed Konrad had returned to his old ways. But his appearance was sober enough; in fact, it alarmed me. I moved to step in front of Lothar and send Konrad off, but Lothar tapped my shoulder. I halted.

We waited. Konrad coughed again, then spoke. His eyes were fastened on my friend. "I still wonder: What kind of man is Lothar Lange? So very interesting! But I can never quite figure out what you're after."

I sensed a looming battle between these two. I felt again the urge to have it out with Konrad myself before Lothar got involved. I wanted only to protect him.

"I got a good look at you, Lothar—that day of your acting up there. A strong performance—well done! Did you even realize what kind of stakes you'd won? The whole village was yours at that moment. You could have whatever you wanted! Say the word, and they're all yours. Now there's something to think about, eh?"

He smirked. "Oh, but you *did* think about it, didn't you? Everyone under your sway! Now there's the idea of all ideas!"

He stepped closer. "But Lothar! I look at you now—somehow you've backed down. It's pathetic; Lothar Lange hardly knows if he's coming or going. You've wandered off course, man. But there's still time to get back on track."

Still closer he came. "I can help you. I know what you should do. And I promise: a month from now, all Rundschau will be ours." Konrad reached out a beckoning arm. "Let's go have a talk, eh? Let me hear your angle on all this."

"*Beat it,*" said Lothar.

I looked from his face to Konrad's, then back again. I hardly recognized these two opposites clashing before me. Lothar was taut as a bowstring, eyes flashing—he seemed a head taller than he really was. And Konrad Eisenstein—he looked small, but at the same time filled with some unknown force. Chills went down my spine.

Konrad lowered his voice. "You don't understand. Hear me, Lothar. I'm offering you…"

"*What—did—I—say?*" Lothar pronounced this slowly, but it startled Konrad. He moved a step back. His face contorted as he sounded a beastly growl. "You think you're not like everyone else!" he yelled. "For an hour, you were Christ! *Hah!* Let me tell you, Lothar Lange, a lot more than that will be required of you! And you should be crawling into the dirt like a worm to keep from getting struck by heaven's lightning!"

His tone shifted abruptly to a piteous cry. "You strut around, stalking this village like a thorn in everyone's side. Why can't you let everyone live the way they want?"

He stepped near again, face to face with Lothar. There was a tense silence between them.

Then Konrad recoiled. He whispered hoarsely, "*Who are you?* Why do you torment me?"

"Get out of here," Lothar said bluntly.

Konrad again stepped back, even as his face filled with rage. "Who do you think you are?" he sneered. "Divine saint? You think I don't know what you and little Arnie do when you're alone? Arnie and Lothar, best friends, thick as thieves. I get it—that's why you have no use for girls!"

This was more than I could take. I leaped out after Eisenstein, knocking him to the ground. I kept swinging and kicking, taking out on him all the rage built up inside me.

Lothar pulled me back. Konrad squirmed away, then took off running. Out of the darkness, he sent one last ragged cry in our direction: *"To hell with you!"*

Lothar stood calmly, his arms folded on his chest. "It's pointless," he scolded me, "scrapping with him like that."

"He's a swine!" I protested.

Lothar's irritation with me faded. "I feel sorry for him," Lothar declared.

"Didn't you catch what he was saying? About you and me?"

He sighed. "I'd already caught it. It's just one more thing Konrad's been whispering about me to every gossip in the village."

I shook my head.

Lothar sighed again. "Heinrich Fleische tells me everything he's hearing in his father's inn."

Groaning, I stepped toward Jürgen Zielmeister's fence and leaned against it. *So that's why the village suddenly deems Lothar to be an idiot.* It's all Konrad Eisenstein's doing. "I'll kill him, I swear! I'll finish him off."

"Let it go," Lothar commanded. "It's pointless. Don't you think the Lord could rid this world of Konrad at any moment? For some reason, He's had some part for Konrad to play in Rundschau."

After I groaned again, Lothar spoke quietly. "But you'll see, Arnie—Konrad will stay clear of me now."

Chapter 16
Bold Spy

ONE GLOOMY MORNING, while the restless northwest wind blew a light coating of snow from the mountains down on Rundschau, there arrived in our main square a cavalcade: several horsemen and a carriage.

I had just delivered a coil of new leather harness straps from my father's shop to the cooper Dietmar Bock and stopped to watch the cavalcade pull up in front of the town hall. The riders were attired in church garments—I recognized the black cloak and white collar of the diocesan chancery in Linden. I saw one rider jump off his horse and quickly set out for our church. Another dismounted and disappeared behind the doors of our town hall. A moment later, Judge Holgert emerged through these doors, hastily pulling on his robe.

The carriage door opened, and out stepped a tall slim man in a clerical traveling cloak—some prelate, I gathered. The judge took his hand with a bow. They conversed a brief moment, then proceeded inside the town hall, followed by two other minor-looking officials who'd also descended from the carriage, followed in turn by a burly monk. As the town hall doors shut behind this group, the scowling monk stayed outside, stationing himself as a guard.

This seemed rather curious to me, and doubtless also to other onlookers in the square, who began to gather closer.

I was about to turn and go on my way when I saw the other rider returning from the direction of the church. Striding quickly beside him was Father Theodor.

Apparently some unexpected proceeding would soon begin in Judge Holgert's district court chamber, which would involve Father Theodor. His expression, however—as I observed him nearing the guarded town hall doors—betrayed no anxiety or particular concern. So why did I feel so tormented by curiosity?

As my mind sorted out what my eyes were seeing, I was unable to overcome my troubling presentiments. In a flashing moment I decided on an objectionable act. I slipped behind the town hall and through its back entrance (which no one had thought to guard), then sneaked up a closeted staircase to a three-quarter door opening into a tiny storage attic. From there—as Lothar and I and Franz Zitterbau had discovered in our boyhood one afternoon years ago—it was possible to spy through floor-cracks upon whatever might be happening in the district courtroom directly below.

Even as I was dashing lightly up those stairs, it occurred to me that for the unseemly deed I was so audaciously initiating, I would likely pay a high price on Judgment Day. This thought, nevertheless, did not slow me.

The storage garret was more cramped than I remembered. Breathing rapidly, I bent beneath low rafters and dropped quietly to the floor. Sliding aside a few small crates, I found the cracks that afforded the best views.

I held my breath as the assemblage moved in below me. Entering first were Father Theodor and the lanky prelate I'd seen outside. They were arm-in-arm, as cordial as could be. At once I felt remorse for what I'd done. If Father Theodor wasn't alarmed by whatever was about to occur, why should I be?

But I stayed put.

Behind those two, the others came in, and everyone took a seat. As an honored guest, the prelate occupied Judge Holgert's bench, the very same one that had been used as Pontius Pilate's seat in our Mysteria. His two secretaries sat on either side of him at the judge's table.

Father Theodor seated himself where the witness usually

sits. Judge Holgert occupied the seat normally belonging to the clerk. Meanwhile Schuhmacher the clerk, deprived of his normal spot, took instead the defendant's bench, where he quickly pulled up a table, upon which he positioned blank parchment and his writing tools.

"Herr Schuhmacher," Judge Holgert commanded, "make note that our proceedings this hour are guided by the Most Reverend Gregorius Delparmo, apostolic inspector of the Holy See."

I almost gasped aloud. Here was a big fish indeed—and representing the biggest fish of all. My thoughts leaped: *The Pope himself has heard of our Mysteria!*

Schuhmacher the clerk began writing, as instructed.

Judge Holgert continued dictating. "Take note also that the Most Reverend Gregorius, whom we warmly welcome, has graciously come to us at the behest of our bishop, although he is not actually a representative of the bishop, but rather of the Holy See, and will send his report of today's proceedings directly to His Holiness in Avignon."

My wild mental calculations continued. The Most Reverend Gregorius must be here to ordain a parish holiday in honor of the Mysteria! And the Pope himself would likely proclaim our miracle to all the world as evidence of the goodness of the Lord.

I might easily have slipped away that moment to rush down and be the first to announce these probabilities to the villagers in the square.

But I stayed put.

As Schuhmacher scribbled hastily, the Most Reverend Gregorius got down to business. He addressed Father Theodor in a pleasant voice with a slight Italian accent.

"My brother, we have heard rumors of something miraculous said to have happened in your parish, and of which we've received conflicting accounts. I'm sent here therefore to investigate these things. Would you, my brother, be so good as to tell us what happened of significance here in Rundschau during the plague?"

Father Theodor spoke in simple words that nevertheless seemed chosen with the utmost care. In his desire, he said, to lift the spirits of his parishioners and to strengthen their faith as a guard against the plague's encroachment, he decided to organize a celebration of the venerable cross of our Lord, according to the traditions of the simple folk, in a performance called the Mysteria. Then and afterward, Rundschau continued to enjoy protection from the epidemic.

The Most Reverend Gregorius nodded. "His Eminence Bishop Berthold will undoubtedly be interested to learn that a priest with such initiative—such boldness—serves in his archdiocese." He leaned forward. "My brother, we are most disturbed."

Father Theodor's jaw dropped. "Does Your Reverence wish to suggest we've done something amiss?"

"Of course not, my brother. I have no authority to judge this matter. I'm only conducting an investigation. Any decision will be made by the bishop of Linden in consultation with the Apostolic See."

"But, Your Reverence—why should our case require any such special decision?"

The voice of our honored guest grew less pleasant. "Why do you think, my brother? Surely you don't suppose an official inquiry is inappropriate when we hear of such a miracle— whose cause you attribute to a display that isn't a customary part of everyday church life, a display that by nature borders on the pagan, and indeed for which no permission was received from church authorities. Surely you realize such a thing *demands* official review. Can you not imagine the potential consequences of your audacious undertaking? The confusion it might cause in the minds of the faithful?"

I saw a tightening in Father Theodor's jaw. "Do you mean to say, Your Reverence, that our love for God should be devoid of audacity? That every time I want to praise my Lord, I must first ask for the bishop's blessing?"

He kept on. "In my two decades of serving this parish, my undertakings have always received the warmest approval of our bishop. I've never once been rebuked by the apostolic administration, and never once violated canonical rules. But our circumstances this past autumn did not allow strict accordance with every rule! There was a plague! Linden couldn't be reached! The roads were closed and blocked by armed guards.

"Your Reverence, three hundred Christian souls are entrusted to me here, and for them I must answer not only to the Linden diocese and the Holy See, but to God himself, who surely expected me to provide aid and protection for this flock in the face of divine wrath. And I—by my meager powers of reason, but with confirmation from my conscience, and the unanimous consent of my flock, putting our trust in God's mercy—I *dared* to profess my faith in this unprecedented manner. I *dared* to beseech heaven as I have never done before!

"And now, since the calamity has bypassed our parish— the only untouched parish in our entire canton!—surely this is a sign that our appeal was heard. Surely our faithful prayers were answered, and that answer confirms the truth: our supplication was pleasing to the Lord, and so also our faith! After all, in the words of the apostle, faith is not only the evidence of things unseen, but also the substantiation of things hoped for!"

As Father Theodor poured out these impassioned words, nearby I could see Judge Holgert's face become ashen. Was he sensing a dark outcome from this exchange? Was Father Theodor setting himself up for an even harsher blow?

After a sustained pause in which the Most Reverend

Gregorius calmly eyed Father Theodor, he replied in words pronounced slowly and weightily: "In our time, faith means obedience to Christ and submission to the apostle Peter, whose representative on earth is His Holiness the Pope. And from *you*, parish priest, is required obedience to the vicar of His Holiness, the bishop of Linden. Such submission must be acknowledged by every true pastor of the Catholic Church, or else he enters the ranks of heretics and schismatics, against whom the Holy See has been locked in battle for centuries."

His pace quickened. "You, parish priest, have seen fit to argue with me. Fine, let's argue.

"It seems to me you took a quite risky step in deciding to act without the concurrence of your diocesan authorities. Need I remind you that the first of the seven deadly sins is willful pride?

"You say the result of your action was a miracle: this village and its immediate surroundings were spared the plague. Yes, an amazing fact! Undoubtedly the grace of God! But why are you so quick to tie this reprieve to your actions—which, as I've already noted, began by deviating from obedience to the Church? When you first opened your mouth before me here this day, would it not have been better to humbly acknowledge your need for the Lord's inscrutable mercy? Instead of arguing with me, should you not be begging the Lord to close his eyes to your stubborn disobedience, and to spare you and your parish from deserved retribution?

"But no! I can see that you're far from being humble. And now you'll see what fruit your injudicious haste has borne. You've sown confusion in the minds of the entire diocese. We're hearing boastful talk—how not even the bishop of Linden was able to ward off the plague, and yet the parish priest of little Rundschau succeeded! You see! Do you understand what is happening?

"Church authority is being shaken. A shudder passes

through the pillar upon which her edifice stands—the inviolability and sanctity of her hierarchy! Has the Mother Church not suffered enough already from such attacks?

"But now, because of Rundschau, people everywhere will wonder: Who needs the mass? Or any acts of piety, or any bishop, or any clergy? All we have to do is put on a little play in our streets, like you'd see at carnivals and fairs. Then God's blessings will rain upon us!"

The scowl deepened on the Most Reverend Gregorius' face. "And so, brother, I ask you: Was it really a blessing from God that came down upon Rundschau? Or were you in fact protected from plague through the intrigues of the enemy of the human race, for his own evil purpose?"

Father Theodor looked crushed by this turn in the conversation. Looking on, I was dazed. In a cold sweat, I scarcely believed what I was hearing.

"Don't we both know," asked the Most Reverend Gregorius, "that the devil is also capable of miracles? Yes—and especially when they conform to his designs, the first of which is to pervert and destroy the Church of Christ, to lure it down dangerous and seductive paths. Our seductive enemy can appear in the form of godliness, he can grant prosperity and longevity and power, he can deliver from any misfortune! We're commanded, however, never to judge by any such outward things, but only by spiritual fruit. And on that account, in the case of this affair in Rundschau—I perceive no good result. On the contrary, my brother, I clearly recognize a bitter root of temptation, which threatens to bring forth great evil if not ripped out in time."

I waited for Father Theodor or even Judge Holgert to interrupt this man and set him straight. But they sat silent in their dejection while these slanderous words of our guest rolled on.

The Most Reverend Gregorius' face and voice took on a

mournful air. "Through this plague, the Church and the world have been subjected to a most terrible ordeal, and many good Christian souls have gone to their final resting place having heard the parting words of their faithful pastor, who never dared to place himself in opposition to divine providence and release himself from submission to the Mother Church.

"But here in Rundschau, though you may have saved the present health of your parishioners, how can I be certain you've saved their souls? Is that not your most important task as their pastor? Isn't the immortality of the soul of greater value than the survival of the earthly body?"

Disputing words flashed through my mind. *Do you dare to say that when plague attacks, we should all just go ahead and die —while Father Theodor commits himself to nothing but our funeral rites?*

Suddenly the Most Reverend Gregorius' tone became magnanimous. "You, my good brother, undoubtedly acted with the best intentions. You're known as an irreproachable priest who has served honestly and blamelessly for many years. But temptation confronts every man. When it does, such a man has a hard time recognizing his true condition. For clear perception, he needs to turn to the opinion of the Church.

"Alas, my poor brother! I find today, to my great grief, that your mind has been ensnared by temptation's web. It blinds you, so that you have no idea how deeply you've confused the minds of the people. Of this confusion there can be no doubt.

"For example, let me ask: What has become of the young man who blasphemously portrayed our Savior in your play? I've been informed by faithful members of your parish that he's now stark raving mad."

Where has this man heard such talk about Lothar? I was deeply regretting the ordeal I'd plunged myself into on this attic floor. Everything I was overhearing grew only worse.

"Ailments of mind and spirit are so often the result of satanic intrigues. Both you and I know this." Reverend Gregorius sadly shook his head. "I myself am amazed that something even more terrible did not befall this young man."

I barely suppressed a deep-throated groan for the hurt I felt on Lothar's behalf.

"But enough about him." Our honored guest clasped his hands. "My mission here, for the sake of maintaining the soundness of the Church's foundations, is to root out disobedience and temptation so they do not sprout into schism and heresy. However, because of the righteousness that you, my brother, have demonstrated in the past, I'm not inclined to impose harsh measures. As I said, I've come not to render judgment and impose punishment, but rather to ascertain the true state of this parish. And though I'm deeply grieved by what I see, I nonetheless maintain hope that everything here can return to its proper course. I assume that the goodness and blamelessness of your past has not allowed the devil to becloud your mind irreversibly. I trust you're still able to accept all that I've stated." His head gave an extravagant nod. "I'm counting on your help, my brother.

"Now—how would you like to answer me?"

Father Theodor rose slowly. I prayed urgently for his strength of mind and word.

He spoke—and the feebleness in his voice astounded me: "I ask Your Reverence for generous forgiveness. I've found it most difficult to accept your admonishment. I admit that in my terror before the calamity facing us, I myself fell into unfortunate temptation, and I led my entire flock into temptation as well. I repent of this with all my heart."

His voice grew even meeker. "I ask Your Reverence to take into account that the parishioners of Rundschau maintain their full faith in the holy Mother Church, as befits good

Christians. They perform the prescribed dictates; they pray diligently, they attend confession and the holy mass. My leadership has undoubtedly confused them, but in their simplicity they followed me, with no evil intent, obeying me as their pastor. They're blameless in this. Therefore, if our case is to be put before a church court, I ask Your Reverence to limit its purview to me alone. Let me, as the guilty party and instigator of everything, bear full punishment. Have mercy upon the parishioners of Rundschau, and give them a full pardon."

My head was spinning. I was entirely at a loss what to think.

I saw the Most Reverend Gregorius Delparmo smile in satisfaction. "I knew my appeal to your reason and conscience would not be in vain. Your recent actions have indeed served as a source of great temptation in this parish, but I'm gratified by your repentance. I'll report this to His Holiness, as I ask him to establish a commission to further investigate the so-called miracle in Rundschau."

He tilted his head. His brow furrowed with regret. "Until then—I'm forced to recommend that Bishop Berthold temporarily forbid you to hold mass, and that he send someone to take your place as a worthy successor.

"Meanwhile, as for your parishioners here—a full pardon, as you well know, can be granted only in a state of full penitence. We will carefully consider what degree of penitence shall be appropriate."

I was able to hear nothing more. I don't remember how I slipped out of that garret without notice, or by what circuitous route I made my way home. But there, without a word to anyone, I hid in our attic and spent the rest of the day in a sort of delirium—at times feverish, at times with the chills. I heard voices calling me, but I had neither the energy nor desire to respond.

I will admit here my own faintheartedness. This bold spy

quickly lost his boldness. What I feared was not my possible punishment for eavesdropping on such an important conversation not meant for my ears. In fact, my mind—so struck by what it had heard—was trying with all its strength to expel this conversation from my memory—as if, once forgotten, the reality it recorded would also cease to exist, evaporating like a dream. The greater my effort to forget, however, the more strongly what I'd witnessed was etched in my mind. To this day I remember the experience almost word for word—so terrible and grievous it was for my soul.

What I feared most truly was any possibility whatsoever that the Most Reverend Gregorius' accusations might be correct—as betokened so horribly by Father Theodor's final response.

Chapter 17

Uproar

I AWOKE IN DIM LIGHT, dazed, with a sore throat and heavy head. I found myself covered with an old bearskin we kept in a corner of the attic.

Across from me, I detected the ghostly shadow of a human figure. I saw it move. Startled, I began wheezing—my frightened voice refused to obey me.

"Quiet, you," said the shadow, in the voice of Lothar Lange. "It's me."

"I feared the devil," I answered in all seriousness, after a fit of coughing. I lifted a corner of the bearskin. "Your doing?"

"Who else?" Lothar lit a tallow candle. I looked over to my brother's bed, where Thomas lay undisturbed.

"Everyone was looking for you last night," Lothar whispered.

"It's morning already?"

"Close to daybreak."

"Who was looking?"

"Your father, your mother. Father Theodor. And Thomas and I—the two of us found you here. So we covered you up, and off I went for a long talk with Father Theodor."

I moaned, remembering all I'd witnessed yesterday. "That Reverend who came—has he left?"

"Long gone. And fit to be tied. He wanted to bring Father Theodor before a church court, but Father Theodor's answers sent him flying out the town hall door like a scalded cat. But now they'll probably send the parish a new priest. All because of the Mysteria. And they say…"

"Wait, wait," I interrupted. "What do you mean—a scalded cat? That man browbeat Father Theodor into repenting."

"How would you know that?"

"I heard them—I was hiding in the attic. Eavesdropping."

Lothar looked impressed.

"But after Father Theodor started repenting," I went on, "I couldn't take any more. I ducked out."

Lothar shook his head. "You missed the best part! Father Theodor asked that he alone be punished, and everyone else be spared."

"That much I heard."

"Then His Reverence answered that he'd spare us only if we all did penance."

"That too," I said. "That's when I left."

"Then here's the rest. Father Theodor said his mind finally grew clear at that point. And he was outraged. He held his tongue a moment, but then cried out that he himself would repent of only one thing: a momentary lapse in which he'd allowed a false confession to be wrested from him.

"He kept going. He said his flock had been shown love and mercy in answer to prayer, and he'd never allow authorities to force them to renounce the Lord. He said he'd sooner lose his rank and his parish and his head.

"He said maybe he was a bad pastor. But he knew how good the Lord was, and he was prepared—if God in his goodness so guided us—not only to stage another Mysteria, but to strip off his cassock and jump and dance in the streets like King David for the Lord's glory. He said he might even strip off his cassock right then and there! But Judge Holgert and the clerk restrained him.

"By then, His Reverence seemed to think Father Theodor had gone insane. He rounded up his retinue and stalked out. But Father Theodor followed him, then stood in the town hall doorway and shouted. He said it's fitting to worship Christ not only in church but also from the streets and the fields and the mountaintops, and the Pope himself could confirm this. But the Most Reverend jumped into his carriage and would hear no more. Then off they went."

My spirits were instantly revived by this account of Father Theodor's boldness—despite what this might mean for his future and ours.

"Will he be dismissed, do you think?" I asked Lothar.

"Who knows? The villagers were in an uproar yesterday, and a throng of them went to him to say they'd refuse to accept anyone sent to take his place. But he warned them about that. He kept saying, 'Submit to the Church, and pray to God...and forget nothing I've told you.'"

Chapter 18
Worse Than Plague

IT SOMETIMES SEEMED TO ME that Rundschau, in the days immediately following our visit from the Most Reverend Gregorius Delparmo, had been stricken by an infection worse than plague. Peace in our village hung by a thread.

Weighing upon everyone was the likelihood both of our losing Father Theodor—who might even be excommunicated—and also of our being forced by the diocese into some action of penance that would surely seem offensive and unjust, given our innocence in staging the Mysteria. At least half the people in our village (including my father and mother) were of the opinion that since God bestowed his mercy and performed a miracle, we should be grateful and never betray our conscience by consenting to the diocese's misunderstanding of the Mysteria.

But the rest of the village—which included especially the newcomers—were inclined to say, "Just forget about the Mysteria. If that's what we're being chided for, let's repent, put it behind us, and get on with our lives. After all," they said, "fighting with the Church will cost us dearly." I could understood the appeal of such reasoning, though I never expressed this to anyone. My thoughts seemed too jumbled.

Meanwhile others, from both sides, seemed particularly heated in their convictions; these differences threatened to become a feud.

For his part, Father Theodor appealed to our courage and called for peace. "Keep your passions in check," he pleaded. "Otherwise it benefits only the purpose of the evil one."

The third day after the Most Reverend Gregorius' visit, a diocesan official arrived to seal our church door shut and to announce that Father Theodor was prohibited from holding mass.

Father Theodor confined himself to his house and immersed himself in prayer. We too, each in his own way, tried to take our hopes to the Lord and his goodness.

For the sake of Father Theodor and all Rundschau, I myself prayed that something be done to put everything right. "Because," I added in my supplication, "no one understands anymore what the truth is—nor do I. We need something, anything, to happen here. Just let it come from you, Lord, according to your will."

Lothar, meanwhile, seemed permanently lost in prayer. I gloomily realized that now he indeed resembled a village idiot, muttering prayers as he wandered the village streets and beyond with crucifix in hand. If someone called to him, he seemed not to notice; he stared silently and kept on his way.

Only with me and old Jürgen, on evenings by the fireside in their house, was he somewhat like his old self. Even there I noticed abrupt shifts in his expression between profound sadness and joy.

Some of the things he said were rather strange. One evening when I was present at his foster father's table, Lothar announced to us, "There's no such thing as a prophet without honor. God has decided to honor us—in the same way he himself was honored."

Weary of trying to understand such things, I failed to ask Lothar to explain himself. By a tacit understanding, we began talking only of old times in Rundschau, avoiding our current troubles. These reminiscences of course were consoling, and we found a great deal to laugh about uproariously. Oh, glorious times those had been, before the plague! Could it really be true those days had forever passed? Such a thought left a bitter aftertaste.

Meanwhile Judge Holgert, Reinecke the blacksmith (who

was a village elder), and Deacon Andreas Vogt were gone
for a number of days to Linden, where the case regarding
Rundschau's Mysteria was being investigated. A village pe-
tition in defense of Father Theodor had been written and
delivered to the diocese.

Father Theodor also made a trip to Linden, returning that
same evening. I immediately paid him a visit. He welcomed
me warmly; his eyes shone with strength and joy, with no
hint of defeat or disappointment.

I handed him a basket my mother had packed with food,
which he passed on to his maidservant Helen without even
looking inside. He invited me to sit next to the fireplace.
Beside me, Father Theodor looked tiny sitting in his deep
armchair wrapped in a cloak—yet also more lively, I thought,
than when he'd preached his final sermons from the pulpit.

He asked how everything was going with me.

I complained of my confusion. "It seems to me things are
much worse in Rundschau now than when the plague threatened us."

"Patience, my child!" he exclaimed. His expression soft-
ened, overcome by compassion. "I don't want you or anyone
confused. So remember this: anyone allowed to drink from
the cup of Christ's love will not be spared drinking also from
the cup of his sorrow. We must, at the least, keep our faith
and hope, even unto death."

He seemed to know my hardest questions without my
asking them. "If that which happened in our Mysteria came
from God," he said, "then God will give us a sign. If our
deeds that day were not from him—well then, we truly deserve condemnation, and I must answer first, for the guilt is
mine."

He grew sad. "My heart weeps for my children of Rundschau, because you're subject to censure when your only sin
was that you loved me—your unworthy pastor—and you

believed in me in your hour of need. But you're free now to choose; no one's bound to me. If it's dangerous in these days to love me, then each one is free to step away. It isn't for me to judge them."

I felt so terrible for our faithful priest. "I won't step away," I promised. Even to think of the possibility of abandoning Father Theodor made me feel like a Judas.

He stretched out his hand to me; I knelt by his chair. He blessed me and kissed my head.

"Arnie, my child, listen to what I'm telling you—and tell no one else. I, too, am in a state of strongest temptation. My heart has been cut to the quick."

He leaned forward. "I know the Lord; I know what He's like. I know His love. I love Him, and I love everything I know of Him from the Scriptures and the traditions of the Church. But what His Reverence Gregorius said when he was here that day—it would mean everything I know of God is a lie and a delusion. It would mean that in Christ's name I've been bowing before the devil.

"My faith is undergoing a terrible ordeal. But I accept it. And if it turns out that the Reverend Gregorius is correct and I'm mistaken—then I want nothing to do with such a God or his kingdom, and I deserve from him the fire of Gehenna and a second death. For then I'll know that my life and my service to the Church and the salvation of my soul have no meaning whatsoever."

Father Theodor smiled unhappily.

"You see, His Reverence Gregorius Delparmo and I cannot exist in the same heavenly kingdom. Our conceptions of Christ are too far apart."

I returned home that night with lingering confusion and apprehension, but our conversation had brought a measure of relief. Some things, at least, were getting clearer.

A few days later, my father was also summoned to the

diocesan chancery in Linden. "Something strange is going on," he told us when he returned. "Our bishop, it seems, has never expressed any dissatisfaction with us for the Mysteria. Gregorius has been playing some kind of game—trying perhaps to make a name for himself by exposing some heresy, and our strange Mysteria offered him an opening. He's been pressuring Bishop Berthold just as much as he pressured Father Theodor. But I don't think it's working. I don't think there's going to be an excommunication, or even a church tribunal. They'll probably just put Father Theodor out to pasture, given his age. And perhaps, here in Rundschau, they'll forbid us to breathe even a word about the Mysteria."

A week later another church official arrived on horseback from the diocesan chancery, accompanied by a guard. He was seen rushing to Father Theodor's house, where he was invited in. Soon the two of them went to the church, where the seal on the doors was now broken. Father Theodor embraced the man, got on his knees and kissed the threshold of the church, then went inside while the official departed for Linden.

Soon the rich, rhythmic tones of the church bell tolled over Rundschau, something we hadn't heard for weeks. We gathered in the church, where we heard Father Theodor announce that he was again allowed to serve, and our church life would return to normal the next morning.

Judge Holgert, Reinecke the blacksmith, and Deacon Vogt returned that evening from Linden in the deacon's wagon. At the church gates, they encountered a crowd of us villagers rejoicing and hailing Father Theodor. The joy of those who had just returned from Linden seemed somewhat subdued, however. We soon found out why.

Judge Holgert carefully explained. The diocesan commission in Linden had indeed acquitted us—but not completely. Father Theodor was reinstated, but only until a new parish priest could be appointed, at which time he was to retire "for reasons of health." Rundschau's deliverance from the plague was declared a true miracle, but the Mysteria's role in this miracle was denied—it was deemed "a righteous act that coincided" with our escape from the plague, but which was not the cause of it. Some precedents were cited: a few villages elsewhere—in the Tyrol, Romagna, and other regions—were also spared the plague, though it never occurred to anyone there to stage a Mysteria!

"The commission praised us for our pious zeal," Judge Holgert concluded with a sigh. "But they don't recommend that other parishes follow our example."

Chapter 19
Closer Than Ever

IN THE NEW YEAR, shortly after the feast of the Epiphany, our new priest finally arrived—young Father Ignatius Schildberger. In his first sermon in our church, Father Ignatius told us this:

"It has fallen to my lot to replace your worthy pastor, about whom there has been so much talk and so many rumors. For a number of years I'd heard reports about his good firm stance for God. Having met him at last, I'm filled with reverence for his devoted service and the strength of his faith.

"And now that divine providence has decreed that I shall continue his work, I've asked him to be a teacher and father to me, just as he has been to all of you for so many years. I, too, wish to learn from his wisdom, experience, and righteousness. I've also requested that Father Theodor, as far as his strength will allow, continue serving this parish along with me. I now ask you to obey him as you would me. Whatever he might say to you—so say I."

Afterward we saw the two priests embracing.

Then winter passed—a winter much like others in Rundschau, though in this one we had to act diligently to overcome hunger in the village among some of the new settlers who'd come since the plague.

Along with a warmer sun, the first days of March brought sorrow: old Jürgen Zielmeister died. For him, the passing was easy: he simply fell asleep, as it were, on the bench outside his home, where he'd seated himself to bask in those warm rays of sunshine. He was discovered by Martha Bierhof as she brought a gift of some cheese and goat's milk. "I called out to him and touched his hand," she recounted, "and he was already cold. His face was peaceful, like a baby's, and wearing a smile."

Many villagers wept for Jürgen—the old man was much loved.

Lothar sobbed. Some of us who were Lothar's age—including Klaus Zillendorf, Anna-Maria Schubert, and me—stayed through the night at his house to help our elders prepare the body for burial, but also to try to dispel Lothar's immeasurable grief. For hours he sat at the head of Jürgen's bed, silently mouthing prayers. We stayed by him.

I confess that toward morning I dozed away. Lothar shook me awake. His face looked calm, even somewhat contented.

"Let's pray together," he asked. "I can't do it alone anymore."

He and I got down on our knees and prayed until some men came to take the body to the church for the funeral service, where father Ignatius performed the rites. Father Theodor stood faithfully alongside.

The burial followed. Our cemetery was turning green with new grass under an afternoon sky as blue as Lothar's eyes.

Then came the funeral feast.

When everything was finished—already evening—Lothar and I remained alone with Father Theodor. The three of us, under a dusky violet sky, returned to the gravesite. Lothar sat on his heels and gently pressed his fingers into the freshly mounded earth.

With a hand on Lothar's shoulder, Father Theodor said, "A good end to a good life. May God grant everyone such an end."

"He loved me as no one else did," Lothar responded. "In life and even in death."

"He died for you," Father Theodor affirmed.

Lothar understood. "Jürgen Zielmeister, so faithful a father to me! He let himself depart, so I might be free to go."

I remained silent. Those strange words gave comfort to Lothar, but not to me.

Lothar rose and stood erect. "I don't know how to thank him," he said.

"Don't shrink back," answered Father Theodor. "Go as you're being called."

Lothar nodded.

They were continuing, I knew, a conversation going back many months, one in which I'd never shared.

In this graveside moment, I recalled one morning in church not long ago, before old man Jürgen died. In the vestibule, I overheard Father Theodor speaking sadly to Jürgen in these words: "I've taught him everything I could; I'm capable of too little." I had no doubt they were discussing Lothar. I feared what this could mean, if both Lothar and Father Theodor in fact truly believed such words—as I surely could not.

As time went by, I clung to the hope that Rundschau's attitude toward Lothar Lange would change—in deference, at least, to his grief, but even more so out of clearer recognition of his true character. In this, however, I was disappointed.

People remained kind and obliging toward him, but I detected also a kind of pitying condescension when they interacted with him. Very few in the village understood what was really going on with Lothar.

One day I was with him as we passed a yard where a rollicking group of children were at play. Seeing him, they shouted what had obviously become a favorite chant with them: "Lothar, Lothar, crazy Lothar! He saw Christ, he saw Christ!" Lothar at once rushed in to join their tag game, prompting their squeals of laughter.

Finally he broke free from their tugging arms. He and I walked on. He seemed entirely at ease with their insulting singsong. When he saw my own dismay over it, he called out,

"Crazy Lothar! Exactly—as God is my witness. And may he grant that everyone be so crazy."

He laughed and pounded my shoulder. "Arnie, you can't imagine what kind of freedom this is. To do whatever you want, say whatever you want—and no one dares reproach you, because how can they reform a madman? Besides—I'm a peaceful madman who harms nobody."

His serious moments were as intense as ever, especially following any conversation with Father Theodor. Once I noticed under Lothar's shirt the same hemp belt he'd worn in the week before the Mysteria. No wonder he often seemed tense!

As time passed, I couldn't ignore how he grew more distant from me, as he had from others. Perhaps he needed such distance in order to clearly view his own road ahead, which aimed for a destination the rest of us might neither see nor imagine.

My intuition of impending loss grew stronger. So quickly my best friend might depart, while I and everyone else would stay behind. Would we ever see him again?

Early one clear morning (it was already April, and the roads were drying out), Lothar knocked on my window, dressed for travel with a staff in hand and a knapsack on his back. He called me out of the house to say farewell.

Everything had been leading to this; if today it caught me somewhat by surprise, this was only because I hadn't wanted to embrace it until the last minute. Somewhere deep in my soul, this moment's approach had been clear to me long before. The human heart is weak—tenacious and full of illusions, even if it knows the inevitability of something.

"Let's go," he said. "Walk with me awhile. I'm leaving Rundschau—probably forever."

That last word crushed my spirit, silencing me as we walked. I was afraid even to ask where exactly Lothar would be going. Would he even wish to tell me?

Warblers and thrushes were chattering on rooftops and among the still bare branches of the trees. On the sunward side of the hills, sprouts of green poked timidly from the ground. We were on the road to Linden, but half a league out from Rundschau, Lothar veered me aside, toward a group of old larch trees growing on a hilltop.

After climbing the slope, he laid down his staff and took off his knapsack. We seated ourselves and leaned against the tree trunks.

On one side, we could see the village waking up. On the other was the road leading to Linden and beyond—across the Schwarzwald valley, across Switzerland, and on to Rome itself.

We remained silent a good while, just like the day when I told Lothar the news that plague had come to Waldheim farm.

Anguish gnawed at me. I again tried to reconcile myself to the inevitable, the inescapable—but to me it seemed far preferable to march side by side into death with such a friend than to part with him, a parting perhaps no less final than death.

Lothar leaned forward and crossed his arms upon his knees. "I'm uncertain," he said, "where this journey in fact will lead. But I truly want to go. And yet I'm also afraid of it. It's like a winter day's plunge beneath the Kreuzbach waterfall, after a run. Remember?"

I nodded. How could such times be forgotten? *And we faced it always side by side—made that icy plunge together. But beginning today, Lothar Lange, we face our fears alone. Why, good brother, have you not even asked if I'd consider coming with you on this new journey?*

Lothar grinned. "Remember running up that snowy hillside?"

I smiled for him. "We got faster every year."

Lothar sighed. "And we're huffing, and steam's rising

from all our sweat. Then right there in front of us—that cold waterfall! Our clothes come off and we stand there. Remember that feeling? Everything inside you freezing up?"

"Everything," I answered. "Inside and out."

"I never once stood there without being scared," Lothar admitted. "But we made ourselves jump, and suddenly we're under. And the shock! You know your heart will explode, and the water will freeze you solid before you ever catch another breath, and you're done for."

"And we only made it worse," I remarked, "splashing out to roll naked on the snowbank, with our skin burning."

"But then afterward," Lothar said. "Remember that?"

"We were walking on snow like it was grass on a spring day."

"Exactly! There's still the icy wind, blowing snow, your hair's full of icicles—but you don't feel a thing. You're hardened now to the cold and scared of nothing."

I took a deep breath and spoke straightforwardly, sounding out Lothar's obvious point: "So today—though you're afraid, you can judge your fear to be groundless." I pointed down the road toward Linden and beyond. "You can freely look forward to whatever's ahead of you—to wherever you end up." *To the destination I neither see nor imagine.*

Lothar's voice became quieter. "It's time, Arnie."

"I know. You've made up your mind. And Father Theodor has told you it's time."

Lothar responded slowly. "My life here is over. It would be worse if I didn't go. If things were up to me, I'd figure out how to stay. But I'm not in charge of myself anymore."

I nodded, and gave my echo: "It's time."

After more silence between us, I asked, "Is all this because of the Mysteria?"

He sighed. "After that day—" He groaned, then started over. "Arnie, you've always been by my side; you saw what was happening back then in my soul, as well as in your own. So tell me: *After all that*—how's it possible that anything in our lives could ever go back to what it was before?"

Without being able to fully agree—at least for the moment—I answered, "It's impossible."

"You understand?"

"Let it be as God decides."

Slowly he picked up his staff, resting it across his knees, his hands in a wide grip. "Here's something I believe, Arnie: that by my leaving, you'll come to sense me closer than ever."

He brought his hands together and gripped the staff more tightly.

It seemed to me my heart had torn loose and was now lodged in my throat. With effort, I found my voice. "Forgive me, Lothar, for anything that's been amiss between us. Know that I've loved you more than a brother. And if God wills that we should meet each other again, your own eyes will see how overjoyed that makes me."

"As God wills," he answered. "And in the end, at least—don't you believe he wills the same destination for us both?"

I added one more statement, my final words for Lothar: "I thank the Lord God that you have been among us, Lothar Lange."

We stood and embraced. I felt Lothar's heart beating in his chest.

"Now I must go," he said. His eyes lit up with the familiar blue fire. I saw true joy there, perhaps more than I'd ever witnessed in those eyes. And true freedom.

He flipped his knapsack onto his back, scrambled down the hill, and set out briskly on the Linden road, twice looking back to wave.

I stayed on the hillside and watched him disappear. I made the sign of the cross toward his journey.

So that's it. Lothar's gone, and here you are. Now what will you do, Arnold Enke, harness-maker's son?

At last I straggled down the hill and turned toward Rundschau, forcing myself into a brave stride that mirrored Lothar's briskness. When I entered the village, it seemed to me in that moment to be a sealed box from which there was no escape.

Hours later, I happened to pass by the house of August Genscher the weaver, who was enjoying the lingering light of a spring evening in his doorway. He greeted me and invited me inside for bread and meat with his large family, all of whom were quite cheerful that night and seemed unbothered by my own quietness. I observed how Veronika Genscher was sweetly attentive toward everyone as the meal was served, and particularly toward her family's guest.

The following day I met alone with Father Theodor. He repeated to me what I'd overhead him telling Jürgen Zielmeister in church: that he'd taught Lothar all he could, and helping Lothar further seemed beyond his capacity.

"And so I blessed him for a further journey, and entrusted him to our Lord's merciful protection. I told him of other teachers in various places, men I know well, who'll gladly receive him and teach him everything necessary and even more. Exploring all this for himself, Lothar must then choose his way. Let it be as God decides."

He hesitated, then told me more. "My soul rejoices for Lothar; he'll be victorious. Yet I can foresee much suffering that his soul is likely to endure. He'll be severely tested. All the same, I'm happy. My eyes have seen Lothar's courage, his love, his sacrifice."

As had mine.

Chapter 20
Let the Lord Decide

THAT SUNDAY IN CHURCH, my gaze went often to the statue of the Mother of God, especially to the crown of thorns—Lothar's crown—with its prickly embrace of Mary's exposed heart. She had seen her Son go to Golgotha, remaining steadfast at his side. Sometimes as I looked at the expression of love and sorrow in her face, I sensed she might also be seeing me off on my path, my own way of the cross.

My God! Does every path lead to Golgotha?

The full truth about this seemed impossible to grasp, yet also impossible to ignore.

And what is then left to us, who must be crucified either to the left or to the right of God's Son? Do we curse him and weep in self-pity? Or do we perceive the terrible mystery of the unity of God and man?

Here is truth: this cross shall not pass from any of us—whether we find ourselves on its left or its right.

Nor could it pass from Lothar, nor from me. This was my conclusion.

What did it mean?

Lothar had left, and I interceded fervently on his behalf, for his protection. I could trust that God would care for him. And yet, what exactly would he face? I ached to know. I couldn't hold back my question: *Lord, what will happen to him?*

There was no answer; only another question. Lothar had left—I had stayed. *Now what about me? Tell me, Lord.*

From the spoken Scriptures that morning, I heard the apostle Peter ask about his friend John, the beloved disciple: "Lord, what about this man?" Our Lord's answer to this was also an answer for me: "If my will is that he remain until I come—what is that to you? *You follow me!*"

And how must I follow the Lord? Where sould I be going?

When I spilled out these thoughts and questions to Father Theodor, he held my shoulders and said: "You'll understand everything in time."

How much time?

For me in Rundschau, a quiet summer and fall went by while I occupied myself with labor in my father's workshop and with visits to Veronika Genscher in preparation for our betrothal. I was regularly in church and confessed my sins to Father Ignatius. I was soon telling myself—with a surprising sense of relief—that my simple life had become like that of so many young men in so many villages; I was merely Arnold Enke, harness-maker's son from Rundschau, and I felt free again to be normal.

This attitude was reinforced by a particular circumstance which surely seemed of little consequence to others, but which pleased me greatly. Soon after Lothar's departure, Konrad Eisenstein also vanished from the village. This time none of us ever heard from him again. It was as if there'd been some strange connection between him and Lothar requiring either that both be in Rundschau, or both be gone.

I seldom had lengthy conversations with Father Theodor anymore. Then late in that year of 1349, our beloved priest died. This was quite unsettling for me, because of something he had said to us while our family was visiting him shortly before his death. Though appearing to be in fine health, he declared, "I haven't much time left. Perhaps you'll bury me before winter sets in." My father protested, but Father Theodor kept on about this, enough that my brother Thomas and I looked at each other with alarm.

"Several times I've been near the gates of death," he informed us, "and much has been revealed to me. But everything is for the glory of God."

He spoke of being visited recently by temptations in which the devil ridiculed the Christians of Rundschau with words like these: "You will die like dogs, just as the heathen do! It's true that death did not take you during the plague, but soon it will get you. There's nowhere to run!"

"Indeed, that's how the devil mocks us," Father Theodor said. "But there are many things he doesn't know—right, Arnie?" He gave me a wink, then kept his gaze upon me. "We, however, know these things—and God knows.

"Besides," he went on, "sometimes you *need* to die—and not just once—in order to understand that there's no such thing as death. But you must die *in the Lord.*" He eyed me even closer. "Arnie, dear friend, perhaps you'll remember these words when your time comes."

Before we left, he begged us not to grieve when his moment for death arrived. "Everything's for the glory of God," he repeated. "And I'll never be far from you."

Afterward, my father told my brother and me to seal our lips, telling no one of Father Theodor's expectation of impending death. "Let the Lord decide what's to come," my father intoned.

The Lord indeed decided. At Father Theodor's funeral, the whole village filled the church, as well as a throng of visitors from throughout the district. Many were those that day who wept for him, though I wasn't among them. My soul was fully occupied with the memory of his recent words to me: *Sometimes you need to die, and not just once.*

Chapter 21
Circuit of the World

THE FOLLOWING EASTERTIDE—in the year 1350—I married Veronika Genscher, and we set about building a house and planning our family life.

And then, that November, my Veronika died giving birth prematurely. Our child, a son, died with her.

My grief was inconsolable. A black shroud of anguish enveloped me. In unending agony I asked the Lord: *Am I to blame for these deaths?* I knew that so much had been revealed to me in the Mysteria and in the days that followed—but then, in my determination to simply lead a quiet and normal life, had I turned my back on my true preordained path, at the end of which loomed Golgotha and the cross?

But if by this I had provoked the Lord's anger—why had he not taken my life instead, and spared my precious wife and infant son? How I wished that this had been so!

In those days, my every thought and question and prayer was full of bitterness. I pleaded with heaven that my Veronika and our son might be welcomed there and granted consolation for serving as payment—as innocent victims—for the sins of a husband and father.

Christmas and the New Year passed unnoticed by me. By winter's end, I could no longer remain in this village that I now associated more with grievous loss than with joy and happiness. I said goodbye to family and friends, and received from Father Ignatius a blessing for travel.

Leaving my house, at the last moment I reached in a back corner to grab the shepherd's staff belonging to Lothar, which I'd kept since the Mysteria, when it had been my "spear." I shut my door behind me and left for Linden—

where I joined the Canton Guard.

For several years my regiment took the place of my family. Military camps and barracks became my home.

In those years, Switzerland willingly sold the blood of her sons to the powerful barons of many lands. The Swiss enjoyed an excellent reputation for military prowess, and many of the prominent courts of Europe would not hesitate to hire us to protect their own domain, or sometimes to take one away from a neighbor. Thus began my wide travels as a paid soldier, my personal circuit of the world. I served the dukes of Burgundy and the German free towns; I also saw service in Italy, Flanders, Alsace, Luxembourg, Bohemia, Denmark, and England.

Although I'd run away from Rundschau, memories from there didn't leave me. One thing, however, was surprising: I reminisced not about Alpine meadows with fragrant scents and inspiring views of the mountains, nor even about images from my joy-filled childhood. I'd think rather of the Mysteria, when heaven opened and approached earth, shining on every living soul in our village. It was as if I'd first seen light not in a harness-maker's house, but on a platform called Golgotha in the village square, on a day pierced by cold wind. In my memory, my loved ones' faces appeared most often in this context of the Mysteria.

In those moments in distant lands when I pined for a return home, I wanted to revisit not so much my father's house, but rather the special time and place we in Rundschau together had entered on that Friday the tenth of October in the year of our Lord 1348—Year of the Black Plague—when I was first a "soldier," and hung my friend Lothar on Christ's cross.

This memory kept me safe and gave me strength to keep going.

I often told my comrades in the Guard the details of the day of the Mysteria. They listened, amazed.

Sometimes I sensed alongside me an invisible loving presence bringing tranquility and confidence. The image of Lothar would appear in my mind. And my mind and heart would ache, because I knew nothing—had heard nothing—of where Lothar was or what he was doing. Where had his path led, in the goodness of God?

I imagined him, like me, in some foreign land, perhaps using a different name. Or maybe he had become a wise theologian or abbot in the solitude of some monastery. Or maybe, like Saint Francis, he wandered about, indigent and unknown, with the heavens alone as his shelter and the whole world as his family.

Of one thing I was absolutely certain—wherever Lothar Lange was, he never seemed far from me. His presence could be as palpable as the quill I hold now in my wizened hand or the light of the candle on my table.

So Lothar was right when he told me his departure would make us closer. Even now, my heart is filled with certainty that when I leave this world, his face will greet me on the other side, with the angels.

Lothar, brother and friend—I'm coming!

The Lord is just and kind. I consider that much of what I've come to understand about God and life and people, I was able to understand only because Lothar and I parted. Apparently this is the sort of gift one is given when suffering great loss. In the absence of such losses, the heart may fail to develop keen vision and hearing. But one must also know how to accept the gift of loss.

The Lord gave me ample opportunity to learn.

When I first joined the Guard, I easily imagined that I might very soon die on some battlefield, and such a death seemed to me a justly deserved outcome for the sinner Arnold Enke's life. But although I served as a soldier in so many places, by the grace of God I did not have to do much fighting. My army years coincided with a period of relative peace in comparison with the war-filled decades that preceded the plague—as if the calamity sent by God had briefly extinguished the flame of discord in the hearts of European rulers.

Nevertheless, we soldiers stayed occupied. Besides having to deal with occasional disputes big and small triggered by revenge or greed or vainglory, we frequently encountered civil unrest and peasant uprisings, for which there seemed abundant justification. Everywhere I saw misery and injustice, the hubris of power, and the suffering of the common people.

Along with this, I became aware of an ever-present deafness, among great and small alike, to the voice of heaven. Most of those who actually stepped across a church's threshold were there only to beseech heaven's help in their daily affairs, as if we have no higher duty to heaven—and heaven has no higher purpose—than to satisfy our worldly ambitions. In people's hearts, the voice of the age was drowning out eternity's call.

As I stood in church, in whatever nation I happened to be, I would look at the crucifix and encounter Christ's gaze looking back to all of us assembled there, and asking, "How long? How long must I be nailed to this cross, upon which I was placed by your indifference and forgetfulness and unwillingness to consider anything other than your own immediate desires?"

And you as well, Arnold Enke—his look would say. But in his look I recognized so much patience, forbearance, and willingness to suffer even more—as long as hope remained. My soul would leap within me, as it once had done in Rundschau.

Finally the time came when I met an elderly priest, Jakob Adlersa, in the city of Prague, where he served in the cathedral. A sermon of his had intrigued me. At the time, I was beset by a number of doubts, and I went to him for confession. I talked about myself for a long time, while he listened with his head bowed to one side.

When I finished he asked, "Are you not weary of running from Golgotha?"

"What do you mean?"

After a pause, he nodded at the sword hanging on my belt. "You're a mercenary, serving for money, putting your very life up for sale—although you don't own that life, and it most certainly is not yours to sell. I'm amazed you've lived this long without suffering a crippling wound that might have brought you to your senses."

Father Jakob had my full attention.

"My son, it's good," he continued, "that you haven't given up praying and going to church. But what's the point of your prayers if they change nothing within or around you? When will you finally recognize your complicity in all the suffering you've observed? How can you be made to see that this complicity consists solely in the fact that you prevent Christ from living within you?"

This brief conversation shook me to the core. I felt a shroud being torn loose from my soul, revealing everything I'd kept under wraps so long and so carefully.

"How long," he asked, "before you understand that your sins were atoned for by our Lord on Golgotha? And now what he requires is that you see others as he sees you—so that you can comprehend his love for you in his death and resurrection."

He let me reflect on this, then spoke with firmness.

"Renounce yourself, my son. Take up your cross and follow Him. Only he who has sacrificed himself out of love—as our Lord did—can understand the law of sacrifice. Already, you've seen so much; already you've understood so much. Why do you tarry in your response? Think it over, my young Swissman."

He nodded once more toward my sword, then ended with these words: "How much longer must you remain the legionary nailing Christ to the cross?"

His strong words staggered me, yet also filled me with hope. They brought me closer again to the Mysteria, where I'd so often longed to return. Now, however, I saw that I'd actually been *afraid* to return.

Leaving the Reverend Adlersa, I wandered Prague's streets, reflecting and praying. I climbed through the trees of Petrin Hill and reached the summit, where I sat looking down on the city below, lit by the setting sun.

My thoughts turned to the fragility of human life in this world. Then I imagined the heavens opening from horizon to horizon, revealing a colossal cross that stretched silently over the world. For a long time I reflected on this. Here was the one thing that surmounted our world's despair, bringing sense to the place where all meaning is destroyed. Here was the mystery of death and life—the guarantee that death is not given final power, and the assurance that life is strong precisely because it is so fragile and vulnerable.

I came down from the mountain at dusk, completely numb and shaken to the core by the many revelations of this day. The only clear thought in my head at that moment was that my previous life had come to an end.

That's how it came to pass that after eleven long years of traversing Europe's length and breadth, I retired from the army, laying aside my sword. I chose to settle right there in Prague, where I spent seven years studying medicine at the university. Fortunately, I was already literate and could read and write in two languages. Also, I'd acquired the basics of several sciences—in this respect my years in the army had been quite beneficial.

The more I learned of the medical arts, the more enraptured I was by the wisdom and goodness of the Lord God, who had constructed the human body in such an intricate and harmonious fashion, and who had imbued the herbs and minerals of the earth with such amazing healing properties.

My greatest and lasting joy came through putting into practice all that I was learning. On more than one occasion during my labors in treating patients, I experienced a sense of sacredness. I believed the Lord himself was hurrying to heal through my hands, and I trembled even as I encountered the foul-smelling wounds, festering sores, and parasite-infested scabs on the filthy bodies of paupers. "This, too, is Christ," I would tell myself at that moment. Even with those who were once proud and strong, but who had so carelessly frittered away the gift of life granted to them, neglecting their health and much more, bringing upon themselves additional suffering and disease; "this, too, is Christ," I told myself, knowing that all must go through the gates of inescapable death.

Years went by so rapidly. When I turned forty-two, two full decades had passed since the day I left Rundschau, closing my door behind me. I'd possessed no hope that day of ever returning—and no desire. But now, I knew, it was time to go back. I was especially eager to embrace again my aging parents, along with my brother and his wife—and his children, whom I'd never known.

It was autumn in the year 1370 when I made this homeward journey.

On the tenth day of October, on a fine clear morning, I was half a league from Rundschau village when I spotted the hilltop grove of larch trees where Lothar and I had parted over twenty years before. I got down from my horse and climbed the hill again, standing there a long while.

Through tear-filled eyes, I could see the colossus of Mount Tannenberg towering over the whole district like a friendly giant. Ahead of me was the rounded slope crowned by the village, with town hall and church rising over the rooftops of houses and shops.

A strong Alpine breeze was blowing from the direction of the village. Along with the wind came the sound of music. Bagpipes were being played in the town.

I jogged down the hill, remounted my horse, and moved forward. Closer to the village I heard singing—choral harmonies with many voices.

Approaching the edge of Rundschau, I saw there a great many empty carts and wagons, along with horses that were hobbled or tied to hitching posts, snorting into their feedbags. These were being watched over by a pair of strapping lads.

Beyond them, I observed the house of Stolz the woodcutter still standing. Here also was a wooden platform decorated with wreaths and colored fabrics. Higher up, I saw crowds on the main street leading toward the square. Above the throng I saw a large cross being carried; it appeared for a moment, then was lost to my view.

The cross of the Mysteria!

Twenty-two years fell instantly from my shoulders, to sink into the cold autumn earth.

I had indeed returned.

With my heart beating wildly, I raced to the two guardian lads and hurriedly left my horse in their care. I stepped away —then rushed back to unstrap from my horse's side Lothar's shepherding staff, which I'd felt compelled to bring with me to Rundschau. I ran up the street to join the people and this amazing spectacle.

How was it possible? Our Mysteria—repeating itself!

The huge procession—much larger than the one I remembered—was ascending up to Golgotha, carrying garlands and banners. And at the head of it was our cross— surely the very cross crafted by the hands of Joachim Vogel. It was hoisted triumphantly by two strong young men striding with utmost reverence.

Before this cross, with Bible in hand, marched Father Ignatius—much older now, but I recognized him. Alongside him were the participating actors—more lavishly costumed than their counterparts had been twenty-two years ago— including a host of legionaries fully outfitted as armored Canton Guards. My veteran eye observed that these indeed were genuine members of the Guard.

In the midst of this troupe—to my astonishment—was Judge Holgert! His gray head bore a gold-plated crown; his robe was white with a scarlet lining, and the walnut staff in his hand indicated he was once again playing his old role as Pontius Pilate.

As I lost myself in the crowd progressing up the hill, I addressed a man walking nearby who carried a wide-eyed young boy on his shoulders. "I'm a visitor who's newly arrived after a long journey," I quietly informed him. "I wasn't expecting such a grand event here. Can you tell me about it?"

"A reenactment of our Lord's Passion," he whispered reverently, "for which I bring my family here from Linden each autumn." The woman beside him smiled at me; she was holding the hand of a young girl.

"They call it Mysteria. It's performed every year," the man continued. "And this one, I'm told, is exactly the twentieth time."

Gently tapping Lothar's staff on the ground in rhythm with my steps, I continued striding alongside this family as our entire procession advanced. Now and then in the crowd

I recognized a Rundschau face from long ago, but I caught no one's eye who might recognize me, for everyone stayed silently attentive to the reenactment before us of this divine drama.

We all stopped at the appropriate places where Christ had stumbled and fallen. I heard Father Ignatius reading from the Gospels; it sounded as if today's narrative script was precisely that which Father Theodor had produced twenty-two years ago.

I noticed again the cross being carried by the two young men. I saw no one portraying Christ.

My curiosity got the best of me; I eased nearer the young father from Linden. "Please pardon my interruption again," I whispered, "but is there no one to play the part of our Lord? Someone to carry the cross alone, and then to hang from it?"

The young man kindly bent his head toward me, quite willing to enlighten me. "The cross will remain vacant," he said softly. "I'm told that in the very first Mysteria—which brought about Rundschau's miraculous deliverance from the great plague—there was indeed a young local shepherd who played the role of Christ in a profoundly moving and super-natural way. And ever since, by preference of Rundschau's people, no one else occupies this cross."

He leaned his head still closer and smiled. "No one *visible*, that is."

I nodded my thanks for his explanation.

The entire procession came to the town's main square, which now, as before, symbolized Golgotha. From his ap-pointed reading place, the voice of Father Ignatius boomed across the square:

> And when they came to the place which is called Golgotha, there they crucified him.

On the platform, the cross was set up.

As the Mysteria continued, I eased forward through the crowd quite slowly, being careful not to disturb or distract anyone. I came to the very edge of the platform.

Listening closely, I heard the Mysteria's words exactly as I had on another October tenth, exactly twenty-two years before. Slowly, once again, the village of Rundschau faded from view; I was again at Golgotha in the Holy Land, on the day and hour of our divine redemption.

We neared the end. Around the square, people were kneeling.

In the proper moments, Christ's final words from the cross were spoken loudly and clearly by a reader. In my enraptured mind, it was Lothar Lange's great strong voice I was hearing: mighty, pure, like the sound of a silver trumpet:

"*Father!* Father, forgive them! For they know not what they do!"

"*Eli, Eli, lama sabachthani!* My God! My God! Why have you forsaken me?"

"It is finished! It is finished! *It is finished!*"

I could see again the sky above us on that long-ago day, when gray clouds parted and a sunbeam illuminated the square, to withdraw only when Lothar's final cry reverberated over us all:

"Father! *Father!* Into your hands I commit my spirit!"

Again I heard Father Ignatius reading from the Gospels:

> Then one of the soldiers pierced the side of Jesus with a spear, and at once blood and water came forth.

Without conscious decision, I rushed at once upon the platform, carrying my spear made from a humble shepherd's staff.

Vaguely, I heard gasps of recognition from some in the crowd. I sensed that all eyes were on me.

I stepped forward and let the wooden tip of my Roman spear touch the cross — at the spot where it once touched the ribs of unconscious Lothar.

Then I fell on my knees, sobbing.

After a moment, I heard Father Ignatius reading our Mysteria's final line — though to me, it sounded so much like the voice of Father Theodor:

> One who saw this has borne witness; his testimony
> is true, and he knows he speaks truthfully — that
> you also might believe.

I gazed up again at the vacant cross — where the Lord himself invisibly remained upon this great throne of his, on this intersection of two beams — this intersection of heaven and earth, of life and death, of eternity and time, of suffering and ecstasy...

Of God and man.

www.ingramcontent.com/pod-product-compliance
Lightning Source LLC
Chambersburg PA
CBHW070559180626
46817CB00005B/1910